D1450831

DREAM TEAMS

DREAM
TEAMS

THE BEST TEAMS OF ALL TIME!

Michael Benson

A Sports Illustrated For Kids Book

First Edition

Library of Congress Cataloging-in-Publication Data
Benson, Michael.
    Dream teams : the best teams of all time / Michael Benson.—1st ed.
        p.   cm.
    "A Sports illustrated for kids book."
    Summary: Explores the history of famous and infamous winning teams in sports history.
    ISBN 0-316-08993-1
    1. Athletic clubs—United States—History—Juvenile literature.
[1. Athletic clubs-history.] I. Title.
GV583.B45 1991
796'.05—dc20   90–46567

SPORTS ILLUSTRATED FOR KIDS is a trademark of
THE TIME INC. MAGAZINE COMPANY.

Sports Illustrated For Kids Books is a joint imprint of Little, Brown and Company and Warner Juvenile Books. This title is published in arrangement with Cloverdale Press Inc.

10 9 8 7 6 5 4 3 2 1

RRD OH

For further information regarding this title, write to Little, Brown and Company, 34 Beacon Street, Boston, MA 02108

Published simultaneously in Canada by Little, Brown & Company (Canada) Limited

Printed in the United States of America

Interior design by Aisia de'Anthony

for Tekla Mary

ACKNOWLEDGEMENTS

The author would like to thank the following persons for their help in writing this book:

Jane Thornton, Milburn Smith, Richard Egan, Jim McLernon, Lisa Grasso and the folks at the Mid-Manhattan Library in New York City.

TABLE OF CONTENTS

Introduction **7**

Chapter 1 BASEBALL
MURDERER'S ROW:
The 1927 New York Yankees **8**

Chapter 2 COLLEGE
BASKETBALL
WOODEN'S WONDERS WIN SEVEN
STRAIGHT CHAMPIONSHIPS:
The 1967–73 UCLA Bruins **1 4**

Chapter 3 OLYMPIC
HOCKEY
DO YOU BELIEVE IN MIRACLES? YES!
The 1980 United States Team **1 8**

Chapter 4 PRO
FOOTBALL
NFL PERFECTION:
The 1972–73 Miami Dolphins **2 1**

Chapter 5 PRO
BASKETBALL
MAGIC IN THE FORUM:
The Los Angeles Lakers of the 1980s **2 5**

Chapter 6 BASEBALL
THE BIG RED MACHINE:
The Cincinnati Reds of the 1970s **2 9**

Chapter 7 AMATEUR
TENNIS
ON TOP DOWN UNDER:
Australia's Davis Cup Teams in the
1950s and '60s **3 3**

Chapter 8 PRO
HOCKEY
MONTREAL MAGNIFICENCE:
The 1955–56 through 1959–60
Montreal Canadiens **3 7**

Chapter 9 OLYMPIC
TRACK &
FIELD
SMASHING HITLER'S RACIST FANTASY:
The 1936 United States Team **4 1**

Chapter 10   PRO FOOTBALL
FOUR SUPER BOWL VICTORIES:
Chuck Noll's Pittsburgh Steelers of
the 1970s   **4 5**

Chapter 11   BASEBALL
TINKER TO EVERS TO CHANCE:
The 1906–08 Chicago Cubs   **4 9**

Chapter 12   GOLF
DEAD SOLID PERFECT IN HAWAII:
The 1964 United States Canada
Cup Team   **5 3**

Chapter 13   PRO BASKETBALL
DYNASTY IN THE GARDEN:
The Boston Celtics of the 1950s and '60s   **5 6**

Chapter 14   OLYMPIC BOXING
A TEAM OF FUTURE CHAMPIONS:
The 1976 United States Team   **6 0**

Chapter 15   BASEBALL
MARIS HITS 61 IN '61:
The 1961 New York Yankees   **6 4**

Chapter 16   PRO FOOTBALL
DYNASTY ON THE BAY:
The San Francisco 49ers of the 1980s   **6 8**

Chapter 17   PRO HOCKEY
THE POWER OF POSITIVE THINKING:
The Toronto Maple Leafs of the Late
1950s and Early '60s   **7 2**

Chapter 18   OLYMPIC BASKETBALL
WINNING THE GOLD WITHOUT
BREAKING A SWEAT:
The 1960 U.S. Team   **7 6**

Chapter 19   GOLF
A SHIFT OF POWER:
The European Ryder Cup Teams of
the 1980s   **8 0**

Chapter 20   OLYMPIC GYMNASTICS
PERFECT BALANCE:
The 1976 Soviet Women's Team   **8 3**

Chapter 21   BASEBALL
THE GASHOUSE GANG:
The 1934 St. Louis Cardinals   **8 7**

Chapter 22   SOCCER
BRAZIL'S THE BEST:
Brazilian National Team, Winners of
the 1958 World Cup   **9 1**

Chapter 23   YACHTING
CAPTAIN OUTRAGEOUS AND HIS CREW:
Ted Turner's Successful 1977 Defense
of the America's Cup   **9 4**

Chapter 24   COLLEGE FOOTBALL
WINNING FOR THE GIPPER:
Knute Rockne's Fighting Irish of
Notre Dame   **9 8**

Chapter 25   PRO HOCKEY
A DYNASTY COMES TO LONG ISLAND:
The 1980–83 New York Islanders   **1 0 2**

Chapter 26   PRO TENNIS
BLOWIN' 'EM AWAY:
The 1979 United States
Davis Cup Team   **1 0 6**

Chapter 27   PRO FOOTBALL
WINNING IS THE ONLY THING:
Vince Lombardi's Green Bay Packers
of the Mid-1960s   **1 0 9**

Chapter 28   BASEBALL
AMAZIN':
The 1969 New York Mets   **1 1 3**

PHOTO CREDITS

DREAM TEAMS

Did you ever dream that you were playing for the winning team in the World Series? Or that you were the quarterback for the Super Bowl championship? Almost everyone dreams of winning the big one, of "going all the way." Maybe in your dreams you are single-handedly leading your team to the title. But in real life, that's not the way it happens. It takes a whole *team* playing well together to come out on top.

One thing all the teams in this book have in common is their strong leadership. Their coaches, captains and managers were all the kind of people who inspired the athletes to perform at the top of their ability. Here are the stories of some of the greatest teams in sports history. For the men and women who played on those teams, dreams came true. Some of the players were cocky, others were modest. Some were big favorites, others were scrappy underdogs. But all of them, for at least one day, were members of the best team in the world!

1

Many people think the 1927 New York Yankees were the greatest team in history.

BASEBALL

MURDERER'S ROW:
The 1927 New York
Yankees

What's the greatest baseball team in history? Many people think it was the 1927 New York Yankees. Before Miller Huggins took over as manager of the Yankees in 1918, the team had never won a championship; but in 1927, the Yanks finished the season with a record of 110 wins and only 44 losses. They were never out of first place for a *single day.* The Yankees clinched the pennant Labor Day weekend, which is earlier than any other team has done it in American League history. They finished 19 games ahead of the second-place Philadelphia Athletics.

That domination carried over into the World Series, when the Yanks clobbered the Pittsburgh Pirates in four straight games. Many people who saw that Series believed the Pirates took one look at the Yankees during batting practice and gave up before the first game was even played!

No wonder. The lineup for the '27 Yankees became known as Murderer's Row because it was *murder* on opposing pitchers. The Yanks had some of the greatest players of all time. The immortal Babe Ruth batted third and Lou Gehrig batted fourth. The two of them drove in 339 runs that year. Ruth hit 60 home runs, a record that went unbroken until 1961 when Roger Maris hit 61. Gehrig added another 47 homers, and the rest of the team combined for 51 more, which made the team total an amazing 158 home runs.

Defensively, the Yankees had a strong pitching staff, and the infield of Gehrig, Tony Lazzeri, Mark Koenig and Jumping Joe Dugan excelled. In the outfield, Bob Meusel had a rifle arm that allowed him to fire the ball back to the infield, and Ruth's defensive play was better than people give him credit for.

Speaking of the Babe, did you know that before he was a great home run hitter, Ruth was a great pitcher? He entered the big leagues as a pitcher for the Boston Red Sox in 1914. Pitchers usually play only once every few days, but Ruth was such a strong hitter that the team suffered when he wasn't in the lineup. In 1918, while he was still a pitcher, Ruth tied for the league lead in home runs with 11, and in 1919 he was moved to rightfield so he could play every day. He hit 29 home runs that year and pitched only a few times from then on.

Ruth made his mark as a home run hitter by slugging the way no one had ever slugged before. His home runs were so popular and drew so many fans to the game that the people who ran major league baseball decided to make the ball harder so that it would travel even farther when it was hit. The new ball was known as the "lively" ball.

In 1920, the Red Sox sold Babe Ruth to the New York Yankees. The price tag for the "Sultan of Swat," as he would come to be known, was $125,000, the largest sum ever paid for a ballplayer; but Ruth was worth it. In the first year of the new "lively" ball, he hit 54 home runs, and in 1921 he hit 59. But Babe Ruth was more than a home run hitter. He was an all-around hitter as well. His lifetime batting average was .342. Only 10 players in the history of the game have hit for a higher career average.

Lou Gehrig was the American League's Most Valuable Player in 1927.

In 1927, Ruth was at his best. His home run total led the Yankees, but his .356 batting average and 164 runs batted in (RBIs) did not. He was second to Lou Gehrig, who batted .373 and knocked in 175 runs. Gehrig, and not Ruth, was voted the American League's Most Valuable Player (MVP) for 1927. Imagine that! Here was a team so strong that Babe Ruth hit 60 home runs and was not even the MVP.

Lou Gehrig set a record during his career that may never be broken. He played in a record 2,130 games in a row over 13-1/2 years. Gehrig was called the Iron Horse because it seemed he could not be injured. Gehrig played until 1939, when a rare disease called amyotrophic (a-me-o-TRO-fic) lateral sclerosis (skler-O-sis) made him too sick to play. The disease caused Gehrig's death in 1941. Since then, it has been called Lou Gehrig's disease.

The Yankees second baseman in 1927 was Tony Lazzeri, a man who seldom smiled, seldom spoke and seldom made an error. He batted

.309 that season and drove in 18 home runs. Slick and scrappy Mark Koenig was the shortstop. He batted *only* .285, a weak batting average along Murderer's Row.

The Yankees third baseman, "Jumpin' Joe" Dugan, earned his nickname because he was good at jumping to catch line drives, and because he used to *jump* the ball club when he played for the Philadelphia Athletics (now the Oakland A's). This means that he would just leave the team, giving himself vacations in the middle of the season. When asked why he did it, Dugan explained, "I find Philadelphia boring." After he began playing for the Yankees in 1922, Dugan never missed a game without a good excuse.

The ace of the Yankees pitching staff was Waite Hoyt. Although he had a sore arm in April and May of that season, Hoyt finished the season with 22 wins and only 7 losses. Another of the team's terrific pitchers was a man with one of the greatest baseball names of all time, Urban Shocker. Already 36 years old in 1927 (which is pretty old for a pitcher), he won 18 games. The Yankees star lefthander, Herb Pennock, was the best southpaw in the American League. Wilcy (Cy) Moore was the stopper in the Yankees bullpen, which means that he was put in to pitch late in the game when his team was ahead, but the starting pitcher was in trouble. Moore was there to "stop" any runs from coming in. Working almost entirely in relief, he won 19 games and lost only 7.

At the end of the summer of 1927, the Yankees clinched the American League pennant by defeating Babe Ruth's former team, the Boston Red Sox, in Boston's Fenway Park. The only exciting question in the rest of the season was how many more runs would Ruth hit. Would he be able to break his own record of 59? Wherever the Yankees played, fans packed the stands to find out the answer.

Ruth had tied his record going into the last game of the season. The Yankees were playing the Washington Senators that day in Yankee Stadium. In his first three plate appearances, Ruth had a walk and two singles. On his fourth and final at-bat in the eighth inning, he faced lefthanded pitcher Tom Zachary. After taking a called strike, Ruth socked Zachary's second pitch down the rightfield foul line. It was going to go all the way into the seats, that was for sure. The only question was, would it be fair or foul? After the ball landed, all the people in the stadium seemed to hold their breath while the umpire made up his mind.

At last he made his call: *"Fair ball!"*

The crowd went crazy and Ruth began his home run trot, tipping his cap as he received a standing ovation. He had hit Number 60!

When the Yankees met the Pittsburgh Pirates in the World Series, they were cocky. New York's attitude was summed up by second

The fans in Yankee Stadium held their breath and waited for the umpire to call fair or foul when Babe Ruth hit his 60th home run.

baseman Lazzeri, who said, "If we don't beat these bums four in a row, you can shoot me."

The 1927 Series opened on October 5 in Pittsburgh's Forbes Field. The Yankees won the first game, 5–4, and the second, 6–2. Game 3 was played at Yankee Stadium, with Herb Pennock pitching for New York. For seven innings he pitched perfect ball—21 batters came up and 21 sat down without a hit or a walk. No Pirates batter made it to first base. Going into the bottom of the seventh inning, New York was ahead 2–0. Then, Babe Ruth hit a home run and the Yankees scored three more runs to break the game wide open.

That half-inning lasted nearly a half-hour, and Pennock's arm stiffened during the long wait. After getting his 22nd straight out, he gave up a single to Pirates third baseman Pie Traynor, who ripped the ball to leftfield. Goodbye perfect game. Pennock settled for a three-hitter and the Yankees won the game 8–1. Three wins down and one to go!

Manager Huggins decided to start relief pitcher Wilcy Moore in

Game 4. Sure, there were other starting pitchers who might seem to be more qualified, but Moore had pitched well in relief in his previous World Series appearance, and Huggins had a hunch that he could get the job done that day. Huggins was right. In the ninth inning, Earle Combs of the Yankees scored the winning run from third on a wild pitch by Pirates pitcher John Miljus. New York won 4–3.

During the decade of the 1920s, the Yankees won six American League pennants and three World Championships. No single team has ever dominated major league baseball the way the 1927 Yankees did.

2

John Wooden is the winningest coach in NCAA history. His UCLA Bruins won seven NCAA Championships in a row from 1967-1973.

COLLEGE BASKETBALL

WOODEN'S WONDERS WIN SEVEN STRAIGHT CHAMPIONSHIPS: The 1967-73 UCLA Bruins

From the late 1960s through the early '70s, the Bruins of the University of California at Los Angeles (UCLA) were the hottest team in college basketball. Throughout those glory years, the Bruins coach was John Wooden, who coached basketball at UCLA for 27 years, from 1948 to 1975.

Wooden's teams won 18 Pacific–8 and Pacific–10 championships and earned their way to 16 National Collegiate Athletic Association (NCAA) tournaments. Wooden's Bruins reached the Final Four 12 times, and won 10 national titles, including 7 in a row from 1967 to 1973. Twenty-five of Wooden's players went on to play in the National Basketball Association (NBA).

Wooden came to be known as The Wizard of Westwood because of the wonderful things he did (Westwood is the name of the area in which the UCLA campus is located). Wooden's record on the Bruins' home court, Pauley Pavilion, was 149 wins and 2 (that's right, only 2) losses! His overall record at UCLA was 667 wins and 161 losses.

What made John Wooden such a great coach? To begin with, he was a genius at basketball strategy and an excellent teacher of the game. But equally important, he genuinely cared about his players. Because he always tried to understand his "boys," Wooden avoided most of the communication and discipline problems that can cause the downfall of less sensitive coaches.

By far the best and most famous player to come out of the great UCLA dynasty was Kareem Abdul-Jabbar, who was known as Lew Alcindor when he played for the Bruins. (He changed his name privately in 1968 when he converted to the Muslim religion, but he didn't change it officially or announce it publicly until the fall of 1971.) Because NCAA rules prevented freshmen from playing varsity sports in those days, Kareem played on only three UCLA teams, but what teams they were. All three won the NCAA championship in 1967, '68, '69, and Kareem was voted MVP all three times.

In the semifinals of the 1967 NCAA tournament, the Bruins played the University of Houston Cougars. Houston superstar, Elvin Hayes, scored more points and pulled down more rebounds than Kareem, but the Bruins won the game anyway. In the finals, the Bruins faced the University of Dayton and won the game 79–64 without even breaking a sweat.

The following year, UCLA fielded one of the greatest college teams ever. Joining Kareem in the starting five were Lucius Allen, who went on to have a long NBA career, Mike Warren, Mike Lynn and Lynn Shackleford. But some people were worried that Kareem was too good. They were afraid that he would dominate the game so that it would stop being fun. Kareem scored many of his points by slam-dunking the ball, and in 1967 the college basketball rules committee actually changed the rules of the game, making the dunk shot illegal. But the rule change didn't stop Kareem from scoring. It only stopped the slam-dunks that the fans loved so much. This unpopular rule was in effect for 10 years before the committee decided that it was no longer in the best interest of the game.

DREAM TEAMS

During UCLA's 1967–68 season, the Bruins played the University of Houston in a regular season game in the Houston Astrodome, one of the biggest arenas ever used for a college basketball game. It was a very important game because the Bruins and the Cougars were considered the two best college teams in the world, and the final score would determine which team was the best. Eight days earlier, Kareem's eyeball was scratched during a game. He had to spend a couple of days in the hospital. The injury weakened him so much that he didn't play very well against Houston. For the entire game, he made only 4 of the 18 shots he tried from the field. It was the only time in Kareem's college career that he failed to make at least half the shots he took in a game. While Kareem struggled, Elvin Hayes played the game of his life. Hayes had 29 points by the end of the first half, but even so Houston defeated UCLA by only 2 points.

After Kareem's eye healed, he started wearing goggles (which he continued to do throughout his long, distinguished NBA career) and soon he was playing as well as ever. The next time the Bruins played the Cougars was in the semifinals of the 1968 NCAA tournament, and

Lew Alcindor (Kareem Abdul-Jabbar) was voted MVP for all three NCAA Championships in which he played.

Kareem was in top form. Though Elvin kept claiming that he was the best center in the country and the Cougars were the best team, Kareem held Elvin to only 10 points the entire game, and the Bruins beat the University of Houston by 32 points, 101–69. In the finals, UCLA beat the University of North Carolina, 78–55, to win its second straight national championship.

In Kareem's senior year at UCLA, two star ballplayers were added to the Bruins starting five. They were Sidney Wicks and Curtis Rowe, who both went on to have long professional basketball careers. That UCLA team won every game in the regular season until the last one, which was lost by 2 points to the University of Southern California. But after that loss, the Bruins didn't lose another game that year and ended the season with their third straight national championship.

After Kareem graduated, Wicks and Rowe carried on the Bruins' winning tradition. The team won two more NCAA championships in 1970 and '71. In 1972, the center for the Bruins was a 6'11" redhead named Bill Walton, who many thought would be even better than Kareem. In '72 and '73, the Bruins won the national championship, and Walton was voted MVP of both tournaments. In the 1973 finals against Memphis State, he missed only 1 of his 22 shots. Walton went on to play professionally and was named the NBA MVP once, but his career was nothing like Kareem's. He suffered many injuries, most of them involving broken bones in his feet.

On January 19, 1974, when the Bruins lost 71–70 to Notre Dame in Pauley Pavilion, it ended their record of 88 straight wins. A few months later, UCLA failed to win the national championship for the first time in seven years, losing to North Carolina State in the semifinals. That run of glory days for the Bruins was over, but those teams—and those players—will never be forgotten.

On Saturday, February 3, 1990, UCLA retired the numbers of Bill Walton and Kareem Abdul-Jabbar. A jersey with Walton's number, 32, and one with Abdul-Jabbar's number, 33, were lifted up into the rafters of Pauley Pavilion. No basketball player for UCLA will ever wear those numbers again.

3

U.S. Hockey Team captain Mike Eruzione (left) scored the winning goal against the undefeated Soviet team in the 1980 Olympics.

OLYMPIC HOCKEY

DO YOU BELIEVE IN MIRACLES? YES! The 1980 United States Team

While the crowd at the 1980 Winter Olympic Games in Lake Placid, New York, chanted "U!S!A!" the American hockey team defied all odds to defeat the heavily favored team from the U.S.S.R. The next night, Team U.S.A. went on to win the gold medal by beating the Finnish team. It was the first time since 1960 that the United States had won an Olympic gold medal in hockey, and sports fans all over the country went wild!

The victory over the Soviets came at a time when the United States needed something to cheer about. American hostages were being held in Iran. The Soviets had invaded Afghanistan, and President Jimmy Carter had ordered a boycott by U.S. athletes of the Summer Olympic Games in Moscow. Oil prices were going sky-high, and the price of everything seemed out of control. Americans didn't have much to smile about until their Olympic hockey team gave it to them—and how!

Nobody, but *nobody* (except for their coach, Herb Brooks) expected the Americans to win. The team had been put together like patchwork, and experts predicted it would finish seventh in the Olympics. It was a young team—the players' average age was 21. The only return player from the 1976 Olympic team, 25-year-old Buzz Schneider, was also the oldest. Nine of the team members were from the University of Minnesota, as was Coach Brooks.

Before the Olympics began, Brooks led his team through a tough schedule of long, hard practices and 63 games. He had been an Olympic hockey player himself on the '64 and '68 teams, and was one of the last players cut from the 1960 squad. After the 1980 Olympics, Brooks said, "A lot of people thought I was too tough on my players. Maybe now they will see that there was a method to my madness."

Behind the slapshots of team captain Mike Eruzione (ur-ROOS-ee-OWN-ee) and the goaltending wizardry of Jim Craig, the U.S. team rolled from victory to victory. It started off the tournament with a bang. Playing Sweden, the U.S. was trailing 2–1 late in the third and final period. Goalie Jim Craig was taken out of the net so that the Americans could put one more attacker on the ice. The extra offense worked. Billy Baker scored the tying goal with only 27 seconds left in the game.

The U.S. players seemed to pick up a little magic after they avoided losing to Sweden at the last possible moment. They started to think they just couldn't lose, and they *didn't* lose after that. Ever! In their second game, against Czechoslovakia, the Americans out-skated the Czechs from the start and won the game 7–3. Their third game was against the Soviets. The hockey team from the U.S.S.R. had been king of the hill for a long time, the very best in the world, winning gold medals in the 1964, '68, '72 and '76 Olympics, and 16 straight world championships.

The Americans trailed the Soviets by one goal going into the third period, but they weren't worried. They knew they would find a way to win. They checked hard throughout the game, harder than the Soviets thought they would (checking is the legal yet rough body blocking used by hockey players when playing defense). In the third period, Mark Johnson maneuvered the puck between two Soviet defenders. He took a shot. It was kicked out, but he put his own rebound in the net to tie the score. That goal caused the Soviet coach to replace his starting goalie, Vladislav Tretiak, who was considered the finest goalie in the world, with the second-string goalie, Vladimir Myshkin.

About halfway through the final period, the Americans began changing on the fly (making player substitutions while play goes on) and Mike Eruzione hopped over the boards. His skates had barely touched the ice when he received a pass and drove a 30-footer into the net. It was the winning goal. In the victory over the Soviets, Jim Craig made a whopping 39 saves. He seemed to spend the whole game stretched out on his belly on the ice, a puck held safely in his glove. Al Michaels of ABC-TV made his famous call at the end: "Do you believe in miracles? *Yes!*"

In its final game of the tournament on Sunday, February 24, Team U.S.A. beat Finland 4–2 to win the gold while millions watched on television. From coast to coast, people celebrated as Jim Craig skated around the rink draped in the American flag. The TV audience could read his lips as he looked up into the cheering crowd and said, "Where's my father?" In New York City's Radio City Music Hall, a show was stopped to announce the score, and everybody in the huge theater stood up and sang "The Star-Splangled Banner."

Captain Mike Eruzione accepted the gold medal for his team. After the playing of the national anthem, he invited all his teammates up onto the platform with him so they could share the glory.

Maybe it was because everyone loves an underdog, or maybe it was because the United States hadn't had any good news in a long time. Whatever the reason, many Americans still remember the joy they felt when the 1980 U.S. hockey team won the Olympic gold medal. *Sports Illustrated* named the members of the team their 1980 "Sportsmen of the Year," and the team's victory made sports fans all over the country exclaim, "Yes! We *do* believe in miracles!"

4

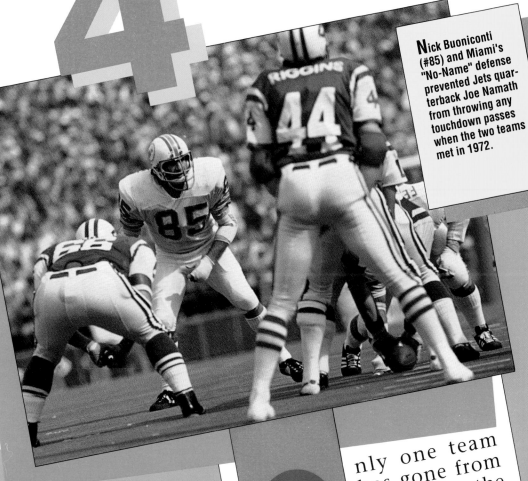

Nick Buoniconti (#85) and Miami's "No-Name" defense prevented Jets quarterback Joe Namath from throwing any touchdown passes when the two teams met in 1972.

PRO FOOTBALL

NFL PERFECTION:
The 1972-73 Miami
Dolphins

Only one team has gone from the start to the finish of a long National Football League (NFL) season without suffering either a loss or a tie: the 1972–73 Miami Dolphins, who had a 17-0-0 record.

The year before, the Dolphins had made it to the Super Bowl but lost to the Dallas Cowboys

24–3. One of the reasons the Dolphins got to that Super Bowl was Nick Buoniconti (b-won-u-CON-ti), their All-Pro middle linebacker. At 5'11" and 220 pounds, Buoniconti was the heart of what was called Miami's "No-Name" defense because there were no famous personalities on the squad. Buoniconti explained the Dolphins' loss to the Cowboys this way: "We were happy just to be *in* the Super Bowl. We were not mature enough to win the big one. Coach [Don] Shula worked miracles just getting us to that point. But after we lost, we knew we never wanted to lose another Super Bowl. We knew then that it wasn't good enough to *play* in the Super Bowl. You had to *win* it."

The bitter memory of that defeat drove the Dolphins to try for perfection the following season. No team ever played a ball-control offense like Miami did in 1972–73. Using this style of offense, the Dolphins would drive the ball down the field very slowly, eating up many minutes on the clock. The opposing defense would be exhausted by the time the Dolphins finally scored a touchdown. Their great offensive line consisted of center Jim Langer, tackles Norm Evans and Wayne Moore, and guards Larry Little and Bob Kuechenberg (KOO-chen-berg).

Carrying the ball for the Dolphins was running back Larry Csonka (ZONK-a). Csonka wasn't very fast and he didn't move well from side to side; but he had no trouble going forward, and he had the strongest legs around. It took more than one man to tackle him and bring him down. Just when the other team began to stop Csonka, quarterback Bob Griese (GREE-see) would hand the ball off to Eugene (Mercury) Morris. Mercury was lightning-fast, and he and Csonka gave Miami a running game that was almost impossible to beat.

The Dolphins started their perfect season in fine fashion, playing the Kansas City Chiefs in the very first game ever played in Kansas City's Arrowhead Stadium. Early in the game, Kansas City running back El Podalak fumbled the ball. The Dolphins recovered at midfield, then drove down the field and scored the first touchdown of the game on a 14-yard pass from Griese to Marlin Briscoe. In the second quarter, Dolphins placekicker Garo Yepremian (yuh-PREE-mee-an) booted a 47-yard field goal. Then Miami defensive back Jake Scott intercepted a pass from Chiefs quarterback Len Dawson, setting up Csonka for a two-yard touchdown run. At the half, the Dolphins were leading 17–0. Yepremian added another field goal at the start of the second half to make the score 20–0. The Chiefs were able to put 10 points on the scoreboard before the final gun, but the game was never even close.

In their second game of the season, the Dolphins played the Houston Oilers at home in Miami's Orange Bowl. The Dolphins had no trouble beating Houston 34–14. Next came the Minnesota Vikings.

The field goals scored by Dolphins placekicker Garo Yepremian (second from right) helped Miami win every game in their 1972–73 season.

Their quarterback was future Hall of Famer Fran Tarkenton and their awesome defense was known as the Purple People-Eaters because of Minnesota's purple jerseys and tough play. The Dolphins knew they would have to work hard to win this one. They *did* work hard and they *did* win, 16–14. The Dolphins were starting to feel like they couldn't lose.

The following week the Dolphins faced the New York Jets and their great quarterback, Joe Namath. In one game that year against the Baltimore Colts, Namath threw for six touchdowns. But against the Dolphins he threw *no* touchdown passes as Miami beat New York 27–17.

The next week it looked as if the Dolphins were in big trouble. They were playing the San Diego Chargers in Miami. Early in the first quarter, the Chargers Deacon Jones sacked Griese *hard* and the quarterback didn't get up. It turned out that Griese's leg was broken, but even without their Number 1 quarterback, the Dolphins beat the Chargers 24–10.

In the following weeks, with Earl Morrall as quarterback, the

Dolphins defeated every team they played, ending up in the Eastern Division playoffs against the Cleveland Browns. The first game took place on Christmas Eve at the Orange Bowl, and things started out well for Miami. With less than 10 minutes left, the Dolphins were leading 13–7. Then, Browns wide receiver Fair Hooker caught a pass and ran for a 27-yard touchdown, which gave Cleveland a 14–13 lead. So what did the Dolphins do? They came right back and scored! Morrall led an 80-yard drive down the field and threw twice to wide receiver Paul Warfield for pass completions of 35 and 15 yards. Then running back Jim Kiick (KICK) ran the ball in from the 8-yard line to give Miami the lead for good. The final score was Dolphins 20, Browns 14, putting an end to the Browns' season.

In the American Football Conference (AFC) championship game, the Dolphins played the Pittsburgh Steelers. Each team scored a single touchdown in the first half. When the Miami offense took the field in the second half, Bob Griese had recovered and was quarterback again. The first time Griese had the ball, he led the team on a long drive down the field. It was as if he had never been away. The final score was Miami 21, Pittsburgh 17.

The Dolphins had now won 16 games in a row. They only needed one more for a perfect season. That game was Super Bowl VII where Miami was to face the Washington Redskins in the Los Angeles Coliseum. In that game, Miami scored only two touchdowns, one on a 28-yard touchdown pass from Griese to Howard Twilley, and the other on a 1-yard run by Jim Kiick following an interception by Buoniconti, but that was all it took.

The Redskins scored just one touchdown, after Dolphin kicker Yepremian recovered his own blocked field goal, then tried to pass. His comical end-over-end pass went straight up in the air and landed in the hands of Redskins Mike Bass. Bass returned the interception 49 yards for a touchdown, making the final score Dolphins 14, Redskins 7.

The Miami Dolphins had done something the experts thought was impossible—they had completed a 14-game NFL season and a 3-game playoff without losing a single game.

5

Magic Johnson combines the three basic skills – scoring, passing and rebounding – better than any other player in the NBA.

PRO BASKETBALL

MAGIC IN THE FORUM:
The Los Angeles Lakers
of the 1980s

There's no doubt about it — the Lakers of the '80s were one of the best teams in all of sports history. The team's rise to the top had begun a decade earlier when coach Bill Sharman turned a somewhat lazy, uninspired group of players into a winning machine. Between November 5, 1971 and January 7, 1972, the Lakers won 33 straight games—more than *any* team in *any* major league sport before or since. But as all things must sooner or later end, Los Angeles was beaten by the Milwaukee Bucks on January 9, 1972. Milwaukee's leader was superstar center Kareem Abdul-Jabbar. At the beginning of the 1975–76 season, Kareem—probably the greatest basketball player of all time—joined the Lakers, where he would remain for the entire decade. (For more about Kareem when he was known as Lew Alcindor and played on three NCAA championship teams, see Chapter 2 on the UCLA Bruins.)

The Lakers of the 1980s became a great team when Earvin (Magic) Johnson joined the team. Johnson was *magic* all right. He could combine the three basic skills of basketball—scoring, passing and rebounding—better than anybody. Before Magic entered the league, it was uncommon for a player to score a "triple double," that is, score 10 or more points, get 10 or more rebounds and 10 or more assists. But Magic Johnson did it often. Thanks to Magic and Kareem, the Lakers won the NBA championship *five times* during the 1980s: In 1980, '82, '85, '87 and '88. In three of the years that the Lakers *didn't* win the championship (1983, '84, and '89), they made it all the way to the finals of the playoffs.

For the Lakers in the '80s, the name of the game was fast break, in which the players move the ball from one end of the court to the other as quickly as possible before the opposing team can catch up. They won many of their games by running and running and then running some more. During the 1982 NBA finals against the Philadelphia 76ers, whose great player was Julius (Doctor J) Erving, the Lakers almost ran their opponents right off the court.

After scoring 16 points off the fast break in the first half of Game 3, the Lakers went on a tear in the third quarter. The Lakers had already scored 8 points in a row when Lakers forward Kurt Rambis stole the ball from Doctor J. The break was on! Rambis hurled a pass to Magic Johnson, who was running as fast as he could near midcourt. Magic dribbled once, then fired a pass to guard Norm Nixon in the lane. Nixon dished off to Jamaal Wilkes, who scored on a driving layup. All the 76ers could do was watch as that basket increased the Lakers lead from 21 to 23 points. They went on to win the game 129–108.

In Game 4 of that same series, the Lakers went more than 20 minutes scoring basket after basket on nothing but dunk shots, tip-ins, layups, short hook shots and free throws. They didn't need to take any long outside shots. In that game, Kareem scored 22 points, pulled down 11 rebounds and blocked 3 shots.

Though their offense was awesome, if you had asked the Lakers to tell you the key to their success, they would all probably have said the same thing: Defense. If the 76ers wanted to get the ball to players

Pat Riley coached the Lakers in back-to-back NBA Championships in 1987 and 1988.

near the basket, the Lakers would force them to shoot from outside. If their outside shooters got hot, the Lakers would force them to pass the ball inside. Philadelphia guard Lionel Hollins said during the '82 playoffs, "We haven't been able to run our plays at all. The Lakers haven't let us!"

Los Angeles ended the series with Game 6, defeating Philadelphia 114–104. The outside jump shot of Jamaal Wilkes was the key to the game. Wilkes, like Kareem, was a graduate of UCLA and the "basketball school" of Coach John Wooden. Like Kareem, Wilkes had changed his name for religious reasons (in college, his first name was Keith).

After the Lakers won their fourth NBA championship in 1987, Coach Pat Riley made a bold boast to the press. "We'll win it again next year, too," he said. Naturally, that boast made the Lakers' opponents play all the harder during the following season, but the L.A. team wasn't about to make a liar out of Riley. The Lakers defeated the Detroit Pistons to win the NBA championship in 1988, just as the coach had said they would, making them the first NBA team to win back-to-back championships since the Boston Celtics did it in 1968 and '69.

During the victory celebration, a reporter asked Coach Riley if the Lakers were going to win three in a row. "Well, I—" Riley began, but he never got a chance to finish his sentence because Kareem stuffed a towel in Riley's mouth! It was a good thing that Kareem didn't allow his coach to predict a third straight championship because it didn't happen. The Lakers faced the Pistons again in the finals of the playoffs in the following season, and this time Detroit came out on top. But that loss didn't diminish what the Lakers had already achieved. They were the best and they *stayed* the best for almost 10 whole years!

6

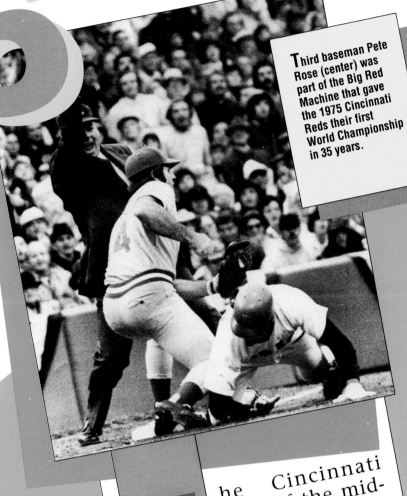

Third baseman Pete Rose (center) was part of the Big Red Machine that gave the 1975 Cincinnati Reds their first World Championship in 35 years.

BASEBALL

THE BIG RED MACHINE: The Cincinnati Reds of the 1970s

The Cincinnati Reds of the mid-1970s had a starting lineup that read like the one for the National League (NL) All-Star team! Johnny Bench was the catcher, Tony Perez played first base, Joe Morgan was at second and Pete Rose played third base. In the outfield was George Foster, who, as of 1989, was the last man to hit 52 home runs in the major leagues, which he did in 1977.

The Reds manager was George (Sparky) Anderson, whose other nickname was Captain Hook. He was called that because he pulled pitchers out of the game (gave them "the hook") the minute they got in trouble. Because of Anderson's quick "hook," only two of his starting pitchers completed 200 innings during the 1975 season (a top starter would typically complete more than 250 innings), and his relief pitchers led the league in saves.

The '75 season was the Reds' greatest. They won 108 games and lost only 54. Future Hall-of-Famer Joe Morgan led the team in hitting and also led the NL second basemen in fielding average (a measure of fielding ability). Pete Rose batted .317 on his way to getting more career hits than any other player, and rightfielder Ken Griffey batted .305. Johnny Bench, another future Hall-of-Famer, led the team in RBIs and home runs. Many people think Bench was the greatest catcher who ever played the game. By the time he retired in 1983, he had hit more home runs (389) than any other catcher in major league history.

In 1975 the Reds led the NL in runs scored by a wide margin, but they could do more than just hit. They could field, too. During the '75 season they made fewer errors than any other NL ball club. They also had speed and led the League in stolen bases.

In the National League Championship Series (NLCS), the "Big Red Machine," as the team was called, rolled over the Pittsburgh Pirates in three straight games (at that time the NLCS was a best-of-five series rather than best-of-seven as it is today). The hero of Game 1 was pitcher Don Gullett, who not only pitched a complete game but also hit a home run and a single, driving in three runs. Cincinnati won 8–3. Tony Perez was the hitting star of Game 2 with a home run and a single that also drove in three of the Reds' runs in the 6–1 win. In Game 3, Pete Rose hit a two-run homer to tie the score 3–3. In the top of the 10th inning, the Reds got the go-ahead run across the plate on a sacrifice fly by hitter Ed Armbrister.

Cincinnati faced the Boston Red Sox in the World Series. In Game 1 at Fenway Park in Boston, Red Sox pitcher Luis Tiant shut out Cincinnati 6–0, pitching a five-hitter. The Reds came right back to even the series in Game 2. Going into the ninth inning, Cincinnati was trailing 2–1 when Johnny Bench led off with a double. That caused Red Sox starting pitcher Bob Lee to be removed from the game, and Boston called on reliever Dick Drago, who retired the next two Reds batters. Shortstop Davey Concepcion was Cincinnati's last hope, and he came through with a single, scoring Bench to tie it up. Concepcion then stole second and scored on a double by Ken Griffey for a 3–2 Cincinnati win.

The World Series moved to Riverfront Stadium in Cincinnati for Game 3. It was a real slug fest. There were six home runs, the most ever hit in a World Series game. Johnny Bench, Dave Concepcion and outfielder Cesar Geronimo whacked three for the Reds, and Boston catcher Carlton Fisk and outfielders Bernie Carbo and Dwight Evans hit three more. All but one of those home runs were hit with the bases empty. The exception was Evans' homer, which was hit with one man on base.

The Reds led by as much as 5–1 halfway through the game, but when Evans hit that two-run homer in the ninth, he tied the score. In the bottom of the 10th inning, Geronimo led off for the Reds with a single. The next batter, Ed Armbrister, dropped a bunt right in front of the plate. Red Sox catcher Carlton Fisk decided to try to force Geronimo out at second, but Fisk had trouble getting the ball because he bumped into Armbrister, who was starting to run to first base. Fisk's throw went into centerfield instead, allowing Geronimo to go to third and leaving Armbrister safe at first. Fisk argued with the umpire because he thought Armbrister had interfered with the play, but the umpire ruled that no interference had taken place. Later in the inning, Joe Morgan lined a single over the head of centerfielder Fred Lynn, and Geronimo scored the winning run for the Reds. The final score was 6–5.

In Game 4, Boston beat Cincinnati 5–4 behind the gutsy pitching of Luis Tiant. That win made the series even at two games apiece. After Game 5, which they lost 6–2 in Riverfront Stadium, the Red Sox backs were up against the wall. Would they lose it all at home in Fenway or rally to keep the series alive?

Game 6 has been called the greatest World Series game ever played. Boston's Fred Lynn hit a three-run homer in the bottom of the first inning, but Cincinnati came back to tie the score in the sixth. The Reds pulled to a three-run lead when George Foster's double brought Griffey and Morgan home in the seventh, and Geronimo hit a home run in the eighth. Then Boston pinch-hitter Bernie Carbo hit a homer with two men on base to tie the score at 6–6.

It looked like the Red Sox were going to win the game in the ninth inning. They had Danny Doyle on third base with one out when Fred Lynn flied out to George Foster in leftfield and Doyle headed for home. It was then that Foster made the best throw of his career. He got the ball to Bench in time to tag Doyle, who was trying to score. A double play! The game went into extra innings.

In the 10th, the Red Sox loaded the bases and had no outs, but didn't score a run. In the top of the 11th, Cincinnati had Griffey on first when Joe Morgan hit a fly ball into deep rightfield. It looked like a sure double, but Dwight Evans made a great leaping catch and threw to first to pick off Griffey. Another double play! In the bottom of the 12th inning, Carlton Fisk hit a ball high and far with Reds pitcher Pat Darcy on the mound. The ball went directly down the leftfield foul line, so Fisk couldn't tell if he had hit a home run or just a very long foul ball. He began jumping up and down, waving his arms wildly as if to direct the ball to stay fair. And it did! Boston won the game 7–6 at 12:34 in the morning after four hours and one minute of play.

Now the Series was tied at three games apiece, with one more game to play at Fenway Park. The Red Sox took a 3–0 lead, but Tony Perez hit another two-run homer in the sixth inning, making the score 3–2. Cincinnati tied the game in the seventh. Then, with one out in the top of the ninth, Joe Morgan's bloop single with two out scored the winning run, giving the Cincinnati Reds their first World Championship since 1940!

That was just the beginning. The Big Red Machine kept right on rolling. In 1976, Cincinnati won 102 games and lost 60 in the regular season, then defeated the Philadelphia Phillies in three straight games in the NLCS. They followed up that victory by sweeping the New York Yankees in four straight games in the 1976 World Series.

7

AMATEUR TENNIS

ON TOP DOWN UNDER: Australia's Davis Cup Teams in the 1950s and '60s

Since 1900, tennis teams from different countries have been competing for the Davis Cup. Whichever country won was considered to have the best tennis team in the world. Starting in 1950, the Davis Cup team from Australia dominated tennis as no other team has done before or since. Over the next 18 years, Australia won the tournament 15 times!

Until 1968, only amateur tennis players (ones who didn't play for money) could compete on Davis Cup teams, and this fact helped Australia's winning streak get off to a good start. Pancho Gonzales of the United States—the dominant player of his time—turned pro in 1949 after winning the U.S. Championship (now known as the U.S. Open) twice in a row. During their period of success, Australia's Davis Cup teams never had to face him.

Another reason the Australians won so consistently was that their captain (or coach, as we would say), Harry Hopman, was so good he was the most respected tennis coach in the world. He had been Davis Cup captain once before, in 1938–39. After World War II he became a sportswriter, and when he became captain again in 1950, he continued his reporting job with the Melbourne *Herald* because, like the players, Davis Cup coaches didn't get paid.

Hopman believed in strict discipline and would make his players pay a fine if they misbehaved. He also believed they should always be in the best possible physical condition, and that the greatest tennis players always played better when the pressure was on. Hopman was terrific at scouting out young talent. He kept looking for players who gave a little something extra when everything was on the line and who performed well in the clutch.

Harry Hopman liked what he saw when he watched Ken McGregor play in the 1950 Australian championship. McGregor was a tall (6' 3") soccer player who also played some tennis. Even though he was unseeded in the tournament, McGregor went all the way to the finals, defeating many of Australia's finest players along the way, before losing to Frank Sedgman. There were a lot of rough edges in McGregor's game, but Hopman thought that if those edges could be smoothed, McGregor held the key to a Davis Cup dynasty. His country badly needed one, since at that time, Australia had not won a singles match in the tournament in four years.

Other players on the 1950 team were Frank Sedgman, Mervyn Rose, John Bromwich and George Worthington. They began the Davis Cup tournament in Montreal, playing on a grass court, and didn't lose a single set (a team must win at least six games by a margin of two games to win a set) to the Canadians. Then the Aussies went to Mexico City where they played the Mexican team. In Mexico City, the land is many thousands of feet above sea level, so there is less oxygen in the air than there is at sea level. People who live there are used to it, but visitors, like the tennis team from Australia, tend to get out of breath. In spite of the altitude, the Australians won four of their five matches. Only McGregor lost—he was more affected than the other players by the "thin" air.

Australia's next opponent was Sweden. Those matches were held on grass in Rye, England, and the most memorable match in that round was one that Australia *lost*. Sweden's Lennart Bergelin played Frank Sedgman in one of the opening matches. Bergelin was beating Sedgman two sets to one when the skies opened and it began to pour.

Play was stopped for over an hour. When the players came back onto the court, the grass was wet and very slippery. Bergelin was still wearing (what else?) his tennis shoes. But Sedgman had put on spikes like the ones a baseball player wears! Bergelin was slipping and sliding all over the place and Sedgman took control of the match. He won the fourth set and was ahead in the fifth when Bergelin did something *really* outrageous. He took off his tennis shoes and socks and played the rest of the match in his bare feet! And he won!

In the final match of the round, Sedgman defeated Sweden's Johansson in straight sets, putting Australia into the Davis Cup finals against the team from the United States.

That final round was played at the West Side Tennis Club in Forest Hills, New York. In the first match, Sedgman defeated Tom Brown in straight sets, 6–0, 8–6, 9–7. Coach Hopman selected McGregor to face Ted Schroeder (SHROW-der), America's star amateur player. McGregor

Harry Hopman (center, here with Australia's 1966 Davis Cup Team) coached the Australians to 15 victories in 18 years.

shocked the whole tennis world by defeating Schroeder in straight sets. Then the Australian team went on to defeat the Americans four matches to one, winning the Davis Cup. As a result of that victory, tennis mania swept Australia. Thousands of people came to admire the trophy, which was displayed at various tennis centers, and all the players became national heroes.

The following year the U.S. team went to Sydney, Australia, to play in the final round of matches against the Australians. The White City tennis stadium had been enlarged and was able to hold the more than 15,000 fans who came to see the tournament. Coverage of the matches made the front pages of all the newspapers in Australia.

On the Australian team McGregor had been replaced in singles competition by Mervyn Rose. The decision had been made by a committee against Coach Hopman's wishes, and Hopman turned out to be right. Rose lost to Vic Seixas (SAY-shus) in straight sets. Then Sedgman defeated Schroeder in the other singles match, but it took him four sets to do it.

McGregor was still playing in doubles competition with Sedgman as his partner. He and Sedgman dominated the American doubles team of Schroeder and Tony Trabert, 6–2, 9–7, 6–3, but Schroeder defeated Rose in singles. That meant that the match between Sedgman and Seixas would decide the home of the Cup. When Sedgman defeated Seixas, tennis fans all over Australia went wild with joy.

Though Australia defeated the United States again in 1956, the future of Australian Davis Cup tennis seemed in doubt when both Sedgman and McGregor announced that they were turning pro. But as long as Harry Hopman was the team's captain, the Australians continued to win the Cup more often than not. In later years, Hopman's teams featured such all-time greats as Lew Hoad, Ken Rosewall, Neal Fraser, Ashley Cooper, Roy Emerson, John Newcombe and Tony Roche.

Australia's domination of the Davis Cup competition ended with the 1967 tournament. After that the rules were changed so that professional tennis players could compete. The rule change particularly helped the United States, where good players turn pro very young. Harry Hopman continued his career as a top-notch tennis coach in the U.S., where he actually helped to keep the Cup *out* of Australia. One of his protegés, John McEnroe, has been more successful in Davis Cup competition than any other player in history!

8

Montreal Canadiens Dickie Moore, Bernie Geoffrion, Rocket Richard and Coach Toe Blake shared five straight Stanley Cup victories from 1955 to 1960.

PRO HOCKEY

MONTREAL MAGNIFICENCE: The 1955-56 through 1959-60 Montreal Canadiens

In the 1950s there were no divisions in the National Hockey League (NHL) as there are today. In fact, there were only six teams in the league. It was merely an honor to have the best regular-season record; it was winning the Stanley Cup that was the true prize. The top four teams in the standings at the end of the season went to the playoffs. There were two semifinal series and one finals. All the series were best of seven.

From the 1955–56 NHL season to the 1959–60 season, the Montreal Canadiens won five Stanley Cups in a row. For those five years, they were the best hockey team in the world.

This was their offensive strategy: The Canadiens put their best goal-scoring power together in two lines (a line has three players) and their best checkers—players who specialize in knocking their opponents into the boards—in a third line. Most teams would combine goal-scoring and checking on the same line. The Richard brothers (ree-CHARD), Henri and Maurice, nicknamed the Rocket, played on the first line with Dickie Moore. The second line contained center Jean Beliveau, right wing Bernie (Boom Boom) Geoffrion, and Murray Almstead. (The Richards, Moore, Beliveau and Geoffrion are now all in the Hockey Hall of Fame.)

The team's defense was led by Doug Harvey. He won the Norris Trophy for the best defenseman in the league seven times in eight years. Also playing defense was Tom Johnson, who won the Norris Trophy the year Harvey didn't.

During the Canadiens' dynasty, their power play (having a one-man advantage because an opponent is in the penalty box) was so good it almost always turned chances into goals. The Canadiens power play was so strong, in fact, that the rules of hockey were changed. Until the late 1950s, two-minute penalties had to run the full two minutes no matter what happened. Because the Canadiens could score several goals in that brief time, the NHL decided to allow the player out of the penalty box as soon as an opponent scored one goal.

The Canadiens had the best regular season record in 1955–56 with 45 wins, 15 losses and 10 ties. In the semifinals of the playoffs they beat the New York Rangers four games to one; and in the finals they defeated the Detroit Red Wings, also four games to one, to capture the Stanley Cup. It would be five years before the Cup would belong to another team.

In 1956–57 the Canadiens finished second to the Red Wings in the regular season standings. Detroit ended the season with a record of 38 wins, 20 losses and 12 ties. Montreal finished 35-23-12. As they did the year before, the Canadiens won the Stanley Cup four games to one.

If the Canadiens had a flaw during those years, it was that they couldn't beat a team in four straight games. They had been in four playoff series in two years, and all of them had gone five games. That was soon to change.

Montreal dominated the 1957–58 season right from the start. The Canadiens finished the regular season far ahead of the second-place

New York Rangers with a record of 43-17-10 compared to the Rangers' 32-25-13. Montreals Richard Moore led the NHL in scoring. He put the puck in the net 36 times, and also led the league in points with 84, while Henri Richard led in assists with 52.

In the semifinals of the '58 playoffs, the Canadiens finally defeated the Detroit Red Wings in four straight games. In hockey, when a player scores three goals in one game, it's called a "hat trick." Two Canadiens scored hat tricks against the Red Wings: Phillipe Goyette, in the first game, and Rocket Richard, in the fourth. All told, the Rocket scored seven goals in the series, and Montreal won its third straight Stanley Cup four games to two.

The Canadiens won the 1958–59 regular season championship 39-18-13. Beliveau led the league in goals with 45, and Richard Moore led in both points (96) and assists (55).

Montreal beat the Chicago Blackhawks four games to two in the first round of the playoffs. In the third game of the series, Jean Beliveau was seriously injured and had to be carried off the ice. Then, in the sixth game, when the Canadiens were trailing 3-2 in the final period, Joseph Ponovost had to serve a two-minute penalty. While

Canadiens goalie Jacques Plante (right) proved that face masks were not "sissy."

trying to kill the penalty (keep from being scored upon when down by one man) Claude Provost of Montreal stole the puck and scored a goal to tie the game at 3-3. Provost then scored the winning goal with only two minutes left in the third game.

At the beginning of the 1959–60 season, fans couldn't help but notice that Canadiens Jacques Plante looked distinctly different. He had started wearing a mask that was made of fiberglass from a mold of his face. Until he donned the mask, he often got hit in the face with the puck and had to get 150 stitches on his face during his career. He was afraid that if he didn't do something to protect himself, he wouldn't have any face left. Plante claimed that wearing a mask made him a better goalie. "When I'm sprawled out on the ice," he said, "I can actually stop the puck with it. It's like having another hand." Soon goalies throughout the NHL were wearing masks—they weren't considered *sissy* anymore.

Montreal finished the 1959–60 regular season in first place with a 40-18-12 record, and faced the Blackhawks in the semifinals of the Stanley Cup. After sweeping the Hawks in four straight, the Canadiens met the Toronto Maple Leafs in the finals. In Game 3, Rocket Richard, playing his final season of professional hockey, scored the last goal of his career. He received a pass from his brother Henri, and shot the puck past Maple Leaf goalie John Bower in the third period. As soon as he scored, he went to the net and got the puck so he could keep it as a souvenir.

The Canadiens beat the Maple Leafs in four straight games, becoming the first team since the 1952 Detroit Red Wings to win the Stanley Cup without losing a single game. They no longer had trouble winning with a clean sweep.

U.S. track-and-field star Jesse Owens won four gold medals in the 1936 Olympics in Munich, Germany.

OLYMPIC TRACK & FIELD

SMASHING HITLER'S
RACIST FANTASY:
The 1936 United
States Team

The U.S. track-and-field team that went to the 1936 Olympics in Berlin was special for a number of reasons. Not only did the Americans dominate the events, but they also disproved forever Adolf Hitler's crazy claim that white athletes (particularly white *German* athletes) were better than anybody else.

Hitler was an evil tyrant who wanted to conquer the world. He became chancellor of Germany in 1933, and ruled for twelve years before and during World War II. By 1935, Hitler had turned Germany into a police state in which his political opponents and other "undesirables" were murdered, people were arrested without cause and Jews were deprived of citizenship and put into labor camps. Amazingly enough, the stories about Hitler's activities were so horrible that many people simply refused to believe them; but Jews from many countries knew the stories were true, and called for a boycott of the 1936 Berlin Olympic Games.

On December 8, 1935, the members of the United States Amateur Athletic Association met in the Hotel Commodore in New York City and voted on whether or not to allow American athletes to participate in the Olympics. The movement to boycott the games was defeated by only $2\frac{1}{2}$ votes, so the U.S. team was allowed to compete.

The most famous member of the U.S. track-and-field team in the 1936 Olympics was Jesse Owens. Owens, who was black, made a mockery of Hitler's insistence that black athletes were inferior. On August 2, Owens tied a world record in the 100-meter dash, running the distance in 10.2 seconds. That score was not allowed, however, because a strong wind was at his back. The next day, Owens was lined up on the inside lane in the finals of the 100-meter dash. Running against him were his teammates Ralph Metcalfe and Frank Wykoff. Also in the field were runners from Germany, Sweden and the Netherlands. Owens hit the tape three yards ahead of Metcalfe, who came in second. Owens' time was 10.3 seconds, one-tenth of a second slower than his time in the second round. But it was still fast enough to win the gold medal.

Both Owens and teammate Matthew (Mack) Robinson qualified for the finals in the 200-meter dash the following day, August 4. Owens' time of 21.1 seconds set a new Olympic record. Robinson, by the way, was the brother of Jackie Robinson, the first black baseball player to play in the major leagues in the 20th Century.

Owens competed in the long-jump event that afternoon. His toughest competition came from Lutz Long of Germany. After the first round, Owens and Long were tied, but in the second round the following day, Owens set a new Olympic record by jumping 26'5½" and won his second gold medal.

In the finals of the 200-meter dash, Owens and Robinson ran against sprinters from the Netherlands, Sweden and Canada. Owens broke the record he had set in the preliminaries on August 4 by running the distance in 20.7 seconds. That win added another gold medal to his collection, and Robinson's time of 21.1 earned him

Helen Stephens (second from right) won the gold for the U.S. in the 100-meter dash and the 4 x 100-meter relay at the 1936 Olympics.

second place and a silver medal. Not bad for a day's work, right?

But Owens wasn't through competing. Two days later, the U.S. coaches decided to change the members of the 4x100-meter relay team. The original runners were to have been the fourth, fifth, sixth and seventh place finishers in the 100-meter dash in the Olympic trials; but the coaches wanted to put their four fastest men out there instead, and the fastest man they had was Jesse Owens. So Owens competed again, and with the other members of the team, set a world record in the event with a time of 39.8. It was a record that would not be broken for 20 years!

The rest of the U.S. track-and-field team didn't do too badly, either. Medal winners included Archie Williams (gold, 400 meters), John Woodruff (silver, 800 meters), Glenn Cunningham (silver, 1500 meters) and Forrest (Spec) Towns (gold, 110-meter hurdles). Glenn Hardin brought home the gold in the 400-meter hurdles, and the American 4x400-meter relay team came in second behind the team from Great Britain.

U.S. athletes finished 1-2-3 in the high jump, with Cornelius Johnson setting an Olympic record by clearing a height of 6' 8".

W. Kenneth Carpenter set another record by throwing the discus 165' 7", while his teammate Gordon Dunn came in second. And members of the U.S. team came in first, second and third in the two-day, 10-event decathlon.

Among the women on the American team, Helen Stephens won the gold in the 100-meter dash. At first, people thought she had broken her own world record of 11.6 seconds, but it turned out that her Olympic effort had been aided by a tailwind. Stephens won a second gold medal in the 4x100-meter relay.

The victories by the U.S. track-and-field team in the Olympics of 1936, especially those won by black Americans, were a slap in Hitler's face and an inspiration to all Americans of African descent. In the years following the '36 Olympics, Jesse Owens received many awards. The Associated Press named him "Athlete of the Year" in 1950, and in 1974 he was presented with the Theodore Roosevelt Award by the NCAA for distinguished achievement since leaving competitive athletics. When the Track and Field Hall of Fame was established, Owens was made a charter member. In 1976, President Gerald Ford gave him the highest award possible for a civilian—the Presidential Medal of Freedom.

10

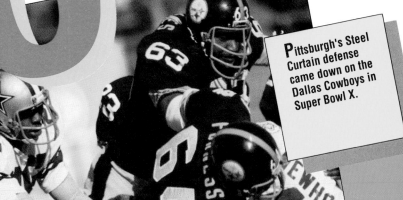

Pittsburgh's Steel Curtain defense came down on the Dallas Cowboys in Super Bowl X.

PRO FOOTBALL

FOUR SUPER BOWL VICTORIES: Chuck Noll's Pittsburgh Steelers of the 1970s

A t the beginning of the 1970s, the Pittsburgh Steelers did not have a winning tradition. Far from it. They had been in the NFL since 1933 and had never played in a champion- ship game. Then, in the early '70s, Steelers head coach Chuck Noll turned the team around with the help of the NFL draft, which is how football teams choose new players from the college ranks. Among the talented players the Steelers drafted from 1969 to 1974 were quarterback Terry Bradshaw, wide receiver Lynn Swann, running back Franco Harris and defensive lineman "Mean" Joe Green.

The Steelers showed off their new style in 1974 when they defeated the Oakland Raiders to win the AFC championship, and earned the right to play the Minnesota Vikings in Super Bowl IX, which was held in New Orleans. Fans wondered if the Steelers defense had what it took to stop Minnesota quarterback Fran Tarkenton and the rest of the Vikings' balanced offense. Tarkenton, however, was 34 years old and past his prime. It showed in the Super Bowl. Tarkenton was completely baffled by Pittsburgh's defense, soon to be known as the Steel Curtain. The Steel Curtain held Minnesota to only 17 yards on the ground for the *entire game!* Contrast that with the performance of Pittsburgh's Franco Harris, who alone gained 158 yards on the ground, setting a Super Bowl record. He also scored the Steelers' first Super Bowl touchdown on a 9-yard run, and Pittsburgh won the game 16–6.

The following year, in Super Bowl X, the Steelers faced the Dallas Cowboys in Miami's Orange Bowl. Though Pittsburgh now was the heavy favorite to win, Dallas had a great quarterback named Roger Staubach, and as a result, coach Tom Landry had developed a new offensive formation called the shotgun. The shotgun was designed so that the quarterback could line up seven yards behind the center and thus be already in position to pass the ball. The shotgun became popular because it was a good play when it was third down and many yards were needed for a first down; but when it was first unveiled, it was a strange new concept.

The Cowboys scored first on a 29-yard pass by Staubach in the first quarter, and built it to a 10–7 lead by the fourth quarter. Pittsburgh's Reggie Harrison blocked a Cowboy punt and the ball bounced out of the end zone. That was scored as a safety, which is good for 2 points and cut the Cowboys' lead to 1 point. Then Steelers kicker Roy Gerela added two field goals to give Pittsburgh a 15–10 lead.

The next time the Steelers had the ball, at third down with four yards to go, Cowboys coach Landry called for an all-out pass rush. "Get the quarterback!" Landry told his defense. On the other side of the field, Steelers coach Noll was calling for the bomb—a long pass to Swann. Bradshaw threw the pass, but he was hit hard and suffered a concussion. He had to be helped off the field into the locker room, and didn't even know Swann had beaten the man defending him by two steps, caught the ball in stride and scored a touchdown without being touched. The kick for the point after touchdown was wide, but

Steelers wide receiver Lynn Swann caught the "bomb" from quarterback Terry Bradshaw and scored the touchdown that gave Pittsburgh its second straight Super Bowl victory.

the Steelers had increased their lead to 21–10.

Staubach came back with his own last-minute touchdown pass to rookie Percy Howard, but it wasn't enough. The Steelers held on to win their second straight Super Bowl, 21–17, making them only the third team in NFL history to win two Super Bowls back-to-back. (The Green Bay Packers and the Miami Dolphins were the others.)

Pittsburgh added two more Super Bowl victories before the end of the 1970s. In 1979, the Steelers defeated the Dallas Cowboys again, 35–31, in Super Bowl XIII. They repeated as NFL champions the following year, winning Super Bowl XIV by a score of 31–19 over the Los Angeles Rams. The Steelers held the record for most Super Bowl victories until 1990, when the San Francisco 49ers won Super Bowl XXIV over the Denver Broncos and tied Pittsburgh's record.

Recently, L.C. Greenwood, a great defensive end for Pittsburgh in the glory years, was asked which Super Bowl victory had been the toughest. "The first," Greenwood said, "against the Vikings. That was only our second time in the playoffs. But they got easier. By the time we played the Rams in the last one, we never doubted we would win."

Greenwood's teammate, cornerback J. T. Thomas, agreed. "It became easier every Super Bowl," Thomas said. "The first year we still wondered if it was real. The next time we knew we would win before we even played the game."

11

Mordecai (Three-Finger) Brown's pitching and league-leading ERA kept the Chicago Cubs on top of the National League in 1906.

BASEBALL

TINKER TO EVERS TO CHANCE:
The 1906–08
Chicago Cubs

Because of the poem "Tinker to Evers to Chance," (on next page) those three Chicago Cubs are remembered better than the rest of their teammates. But that poem doesn't tell the whole story. The *team* is worth remembering, too. Between 1906 and 1910 the Cubs won four National League pennants

DREAM TEAMS

These are the saddest of possible words,
Tinker-to-Evers-to-Chance.
Trio of Bear Cubs fleeter than birds,
Tinker-to-Evers-to-Chance.
Pricking our gonfalon bubble,
Making a Giant hit into a double,
Words that are weighty with nothing but trouble,
Tinker-to-Evers-to-Chance.

—Franklin P. Adams
A New York Giants fan

(in 1906, '07, '08 and '10) and two World Championships.

In 1906, they won 116 of the 152 games they played. That's a winning percentage of .763, the best major league win-loss record of the 20th Century! And in 1909, the one year during that stretch when the Cubs failed to win the pennant, they won a fantastic 104 games. But they finished second to the Pittsburgh Pirates and their superstar shortstop Honus Wagner.

In 1906, the trio of Tinker, Evers and Chance hardly seemed worthy of poetry. Chicago shortstop Joe Tinker batted a puny .233. Johnny Evers led the National League second basemen in errors that year with 44. Frank Chance, the Cubs first baseman and manager, was known more for hitting—his batting average was .319—than for his fielding. Tinker to Evers to Chance accounted for only eight double plays in all of 1906. Evers to Tinker to Chance turned over another nine, nowhere near the league lead.

Chicago's third baseman was actually more noteworthy than any of the famous three. His name was Harry Steinfeldt. He batted .327 in 1906, led the National League third basemen in fielding average (a measure of fielding ability), and led the league in RBIs with 83. Yet history has all but forgotten him. Why? Because he wasn't in the poem.

The Cubs led the National League in batting that year with an average of .262. The real reason, however, that the Cubs won so many games was their league-leading earned run average (ERA). Their pitchers combined for an ERA of 1.76. The ace of the staff was Mordecai (Three-Finger) Brown, who had only three fingers on his pitching hand because of a childhood accident. In 1906, Brown won 26 games and lost only 6 and had a league-leading ERA of 1.04.

In 1907 the Cubs won the World Series four games to none with one tie over the Detroit Tigers. That's right—a *tie*. The opening game was called because of darkness with the score 3–3. That outcome was fairly common in the days before lighted ballparks.

The Cubs won the National League pennant in 1908 only because a lot of strange things happened. All year long the New York Giants and the Cubs had been battling for the league lead. Late in the season, the Cubs came to the Giants' home ballpark, the Polo Grounds in New York, for the most important series of the year. Chicago won the first two games. In Game 3 the first run wasn't scored until the top of the fifth inning when Tinker hit a line drive past Giants outfielder Mike Donlin for an inside-the-park home run. But Donlin tied the score in the bottom of the fifth by knocking in a run with a single.

The score remained 1–1 until the bottom of the ninth, when rookie Fred Merkle came up to bat for the Giants. There were two men out

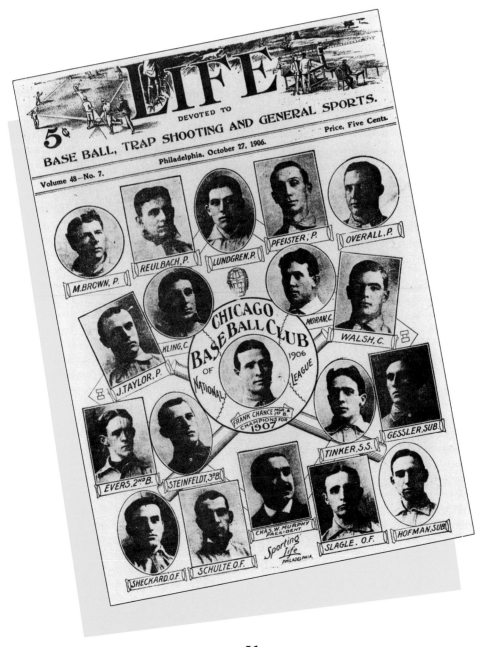

and a man on first. Merkle smacked a single. Now New York had men on first and third and Al Bridwell was up. He rapped out another single, and the crowd roared and began to charge onto the field as the "winning" run crossed the plate.

But it didn't turn out to be the winning run after all. The rules say that a run cannot score if the final out of the inning comes on a force play. Merkle had not run to second base. Instead he ran out to centerfield to avoid being trampled by the crowd. The Cubs got the ball back and threw it to Evers, who was standing on second base. Merkle was out, and the winning run didn't score. The game couldn't start up again because the angry Giants fans were rioting on the field, so it was decided that the score would remain 1–1, and the game would be replayed at the end of the season if necessary.

It *was* necessary. The Giants and the Cubs both finished the regular season with a 98–55 record.

For the rematch, the largest crowd ever to see a baseball game gathered at the Polo Grounds. Before the game started, somebody set fire to a portion of the outfield fence and when it had burned to the ground, fans who had been stuck outside charged onto the field so they could watch the action close-up. When the Cubs won the game 4–2, earning their third straight National League pennant, Giants fans were furious. They stormed onto the field and attacked the Cubs players. Frank Chance was smacked in the throat and another player was slashed with a knife. Who would have guessed that baseball could be so dangerous?

In the 1908 World Series, the Cubs defeated the Detroit Tigers once again, four games to one. In their one victory, the Tigers were fueled by Ty Cobb's four-hit attack. Orval Overall of the Cubs pitched two complete games, giving up only one run, and Three-Finger Brown pitched a complete game shutout in Game 4.

The team from the North Side of Chicago was still Number 1!

The gallery at golf's Canada Cup in 1964 was all for Arnold Palmer even though he was just one of the four players on the American team.

GOLF

DEAD SOLID PERFECT IN HAWAII: The 1964 United States Canada Cup Team

Golf's Canada Cup (now known as the World Cup) was first held in 1953. It was begun to promote goodwill among nations. Even though most of the golfers were professionals who were accustomed to making thousands of dollars at their sport, no money went to the winner of this tournament. These players competed for national honor and pride, not for cash. The team with the lowest combined score got to take the gold-plated cup home on behalf of its country.

In 1964, the matches were held at the Royal Kaanapali Golf Course on the beautiful island of Maui, Hawaii. Golfers from 34 countries entered the competition. The American team consisted of Arnold Palmer, Jack Nicklaus, and two Hawaiian players, Ted Makalena and Paul Scodeller. The '64 Canada Cup was the first major sports tournament ever to be held in Hawaii, and there was an easy, relaxed feeling among the players that is never found during Professional Golf Association tournaments.

All that vacation feeling evaporated as soon as the tournament began. From the way Nicklaus and Palmer played, you would have thought they were playing for a million dollars. Although they were teammates instead of competitors, each man felt a strong urge to beat the other. They were the two best golfers in the world; the big question was who was Number 1 and who was Number 2.

Palmer came into the tournament with a hot hand. In a preliminary pro-am (professionals paired with amateurs) competition, he shot the best round anyone had ever played on the Royal Kaanapali links, shooting a 7-under-par 65 on the 7,200-yard course. That means he took 65 strokes to complete the 18 holes of the course when a top golfer would be expected to take 72, which is par. His drives were dead solid perfect, and his putts dropped easily into the hole, despite the fact that his putting had been giving him some trouble in the weeks before his trip to Hawaii. None of the other players were putting well at all, however, and many of them were complaining about the greens. The Royal Kaanapali greens were planted with a kind of grass called Seaside Bent, which had been developed to withstand salt air and mist, conditions that kill most grass. The Seaside Bent stayed healthy, all right, but it tended to get bumpy from the spikes on the golfers' shoes. This made it difficult to put the ball straight into the hole.

The grass obviously didn't bother Palmer. He said, "The reason I like these greens is because you know just how the ball is going to behave."

Palmer played brilliantly and the crowds of spectators grew bigger and bigger as his dazzling play continued. Palmer shot 66, 67, 67 in the first three rounds and was 16 strokes under par going into the final round. He was known for being very serious when he played golf, but by the third round he was feeling pretty relaxed. As Arnie was walking down a fairway on the back nine, he heard some Hawaiian music and did a little hula dance for the crowd. This delighted his followers, who were called "Arnie's Army."

Jack Nicklaus was playing well, too. On Saturday, he shot a 65, tying the course record his teammate had set three days earlier. After three rounds, Nicklaus was 10 under par, and the U.S. team as a whole was 26 under par, 9 strokes ahead of the South African team of Gary Player and Denis Hutchinson, which was in second place.

When the Americans and South Africans were paired for the final round, the gallery following the foursome had grown to more than 7,000 fans! Most of them were there to watch Arnold Palmer. He and Nicklaus might have been competing to find out who was the better golfer, but when it came to popularity, there was no contest. Nicklaus was a good sport about it, though. When he saw the huge number of people, many of whom were carrying "Arnie's Army" signs, he joked, "How did they all get here? Swim?"

The final round of the tournament took more than six hours to play (a normal round usually lasts about four hours). The slow pace began to upset Palmer, and his score ballooned to 78. One day he was hot, and the next day he was not. All of a sudden it seemed he couldn't do anything right. Nicklaus, however, picked up the slack and was able to turn in a tough score of 70. It was a difficult 70 because he drove into the water off the 15th tee and 3-putted the 16th green, which means that after he got the ball on the green, it took him three putts to get it into the hole; the average, or par, is two putts.

Despite Palmer's letdown, the team's earlier play had been so superb that victory in the tournament was assured, and the Americans ended up winning by 11 strokes over second-place Argentina. The South Africans did so poorly in the final round that they lost second place. Because of Palmer's high score in the last round, Nicklaus had the lowest overall score. But Palmer and Nicklaus' combined score of 554 for the 4 rounds shattered the tournament record for team play. The Canada Cup was in U.S. hands for the fifth straight year.

13

Red Auerbach coached the Boston Celtics to their first NBA Championship in 1957, and then eight in a row beginning in 1959.

BOSTON CELTICS
NBA
1957 WORLD CHAMPIONS

BOSTON CELTICS
NBA
1981 WORLD CHAMPIONS

PRO BASKETBALL

DYNASTY IN THE GARDEN:
The Boston Celtics of the 1950s and '60s

No professional team in history has ever dominated a sport for more than a decade the way the Boston Celtics dominated the NBA from 1957 to 1969. In those 13 years, the Celtics won 11 championships, and in the 1959–60 season, they lost only two games on their home court in the Boston Garden all year.

The Celtics coach from 1950 to 1966 was Red Auerbach (OW-er-bock), who won more NBA games than any other coach. Though Coach Auerbach had plenty of talent to work with, he deserves a lot of credit for keeping his teams sharp over the years. Some teams with a lot of talent get lazy or bored after a few years of playing championship ball, but this never happened to the Celtics. Sometimes repeat-championship teams develop problems in the locker room as personality conflicts arise among the players, but this never happened to the Celtics, either. They were good sports and good teammates.

It was no accident that the Celtics *forgot* how to lose in 1956, the same year superstar center Bill Russell joined the team. The starting five for Boston in 1956–57 were Bill Sharman, Bob Cousy, Tommy Heinsohn, Jim Loscutoff and Bill Russell. Twelve years later, the starting five had changed to John (Hondo) Havlicek, Bailey Howell, Sam Jones, Larry Siegfried—and Bill Russell. Russell was the only player the 1956–57 and 1968–69 Celtics had in common. During those 13 full seasons, the Celtics won 672 games and lost only 271, and Russell led the NBA in rebounding four times, making him second on the list of career rebounds behind Wilt (The Stilt) Chamberlain.

Russell's game was defense. He was never as much of a scorer as Chamberlain was. Russell's job was to keep the other team from scoring and he did it better than anybody else. Whenever Russell's team played against Chamberlain's the two big men would have a memorable battle on the court.

Russell and Chamberlain first played against each other during Chamberlain's rookie season with the Philadelphia Warriors in 1959-60. They did not like each other. It was the beginning of a rivalry that would continue throughout their careers. In their first playoff meeting that season, Chamberlain scored 235 points for the Warriors in six games, and Russell scored only 154 for the Celtics. But Boston had the stronger team and beat the Warriors, then went on to beat St. Louis for the NBA Championship.

Russell and Chamberlain next met in the playoffs in 1962. The series went the full seven games and was the first of four seventh-game showdowns that put Russell up against Wilt. The Warriors were ahead in the third quarter of the final game, but the Celtics went on a scoring streak and pulled ahead by 10 points halfway through the final quarter. Though a 3-point play by Wilt tied the game with 16 seconds left, the Celtics Sam Jones hit a jumper to win the series. The Celtics then went on to beat the Los Angeles Lakers in the finals and won their fourth consecutive NBA championship.

In 1964, the Celtics met the Warriors in the playoffs again, but this

When Wilt Chamberlain and Bill Russell first met on the court in 1959, the two great centers began a rivalry that continued throughout their careers.

time it was in the finals. (The Warriors had moved to San Francisco.) Although Chamberlain scored more points and had more rebounds, Russell and the Celtics won the championship in only five games. The following season, when the Celtics defeated the Philadelphia 76ers in the playoff semifinals, it was *still* Russell versus Chamberlain because Wilt had been traded from the Warriors to the 76ers.

Chamberlain finally got his revenge in the 1967 semifinals when the 76ers eliminated the Celtics from the playoffs, winning in five games. The victory was doubly sweet for Chamberlain because, by this time, Russell had become the Celtics coach, as well as their center.

The Celtics and the 76ers met again in the 1968 semifinals. Bill Russell was 34 years old, and he was beginning to slow down. But he proved that when it counted, he was as good as ever. In Game 7 of that series, with 34 seconds left, Russell made a free throw, increasing Boston's lead from 2 to 3 points. Philadelphia's Chet Walker tried to drive to the basket, but Russell blocked Chet's shot. The 76ers grabbed the loose ball, shot again—and missed. Russell hauled in the rebound.

Celtics free throws in the final seconds completed the scoring, and the Celtics won the game 100-96.

The 1968–69 season was Russell's last as a player and he faced Chamberlain, who was now playing for the Los Angeles Lakers, in his very last game. In the fourth quarter of Game 7 of the finals, the Celtics were ahead by 13 points. With 5:45 left, Chamberlain injured his foot and limped off the floor. Wilt never went back into the game. Instead, he watched from the bench as the Celtics won by 2 points, 108-106. Wilt would never get another chance to beat Bill Russell.

Here is a list of Celtics' records in NBA playoff finals between 1959 and 1969. All were best of seven series:

> 1959 — Boston 4, Minneapolis 0
> 1960 — Boston 4, St. Louis 3
> 1961 — Boston 4, St. Louis 1
> 1962 — Boston 4, Los Angeles 3
> 1963 — Boston 4, Los Angeles 2
> 1964 — Boston 4, San Francisco 1
> 1965 — Boston 4, Los Angeles 1
> 1966 — Boston 4, Los Angeles 3
> 1968 — Boston 4, Los Angeles 2
> 1969 — Boston 4, Los Angeles 3

WOW !

14

Light-heavyweight boxer Leon Spinks surprised the world in the 1976 Montreal Olympics by defeating Cuba's Sixto Soria for the gold.

OLYMPIC BOXING

A TEAM OF FUTURE CHAMPIONS: The 1976 United States Team

The success of the United States boxing team in the 1976 Olympics took everybody by surprise. Going into the Games, which were held in Montreal, only one American boxer, "Sugar Ray" Leonard, was expected to bring home the gold. Sugar Ray, who was only 20 years old, breezed through the

Olympic trials (a tournament held to decide who would be on the U.S. Olympic team). He was a light-welterweight, which means that he had to weigh less than 140 pounds to box. The trials were held in Cincinnati's Riverfront Stadium several months before the '76 Games. Going into the trials, Leonard had a record of 127 wins and only 5 losses. He had been knocked off his feet in the ring just once, but he immediately got up and knocked out his opponent.

Even before the Olympics began, AAU boxing chairman and Olympic coach Rolly Schwartz was calling Leonard "the greatest amateur I've seen in 38 years of boxing. He has the fastest reflexes and the greatest balance. Reflexes like Muhammed Ali, balance like Sugar Ray Robinson [the famous middleweight boxer after whom Leonard was nicknamed]. He can take you out with either hand. He's got a jab that will take your head and set it back in fifth row. Right now he could beat any lightweight or welterweight in the world, amateur or professional."

Among those who made the team but were *not* expected to win a gold medal were the Spinks brothers from St. Louis, Missouri. At 23, Leon Spinks was the older (by three years) and the heavier of the two. He was a light-heavyweight (less than 179 pounds) who had won a bronze medal at the World Games in Havana and a silver medal at the Pan-American Games held in Mexico City in 1975. Leon's younger brother, Michael, was not as highly regarded, but he won a spot on the Olympic team in the middleweight class (less than 165$\frac{1}{2}$ pounds).

The surprise of the Olympic trials was heavyweight (less than 200$\frac{1}{2}$ pounds) "Big John" Tate. Tate had been boxing for only 19 months when he pounded his way on to the Olympic squad. Though he lacked skill, he was very strong. Other members of the team included lightweight (less than 132 pounds) Howard (John-John) Davis and bantamweight (less than 119$\frac{1}{2}$ pounds) Charles Mooney.

In the finals of the '76 Olympics, Leon Spinks' "little" brother Michael faced Rufat Riskiev, the only boxer from the Soviet Union to make it into the final round. Michael gave Riskiev such a fierce beating that with little more than a minute to go in the third and final round, Riskiev quit. Spinks' last punch was to Riskiev's belly, forcing him to double over. Riskiev claimed that the punch had been below the belt, but the referee didn't agree. Michael was declared the winner.

Leon Spinks' fight against Cuba's Sixto Soria came right after Michael's bout. Both boxers threw a lot of punches, but Spinks hit harder. Less than a minute into the third and final round, a long right hook by Spinks to Soria's temple put the Cuban down on his face. Soria made it to his feet before the referee had counted to 10, but he was in no condition to continue the fight, and Spinks won by a TKO (technical knockout). Leon's victory was the biggest upset of the games because Soria had been considered the favorite to win the gold.

Leo Randolph, an 18-year-old high school senior from Tacoma, Washington, won the gold medal in the flyweight class (112$\frac{1}{2}$ pounds). John-John Davis brought home the gold in the lightweight division by defeating a Romanian named Simion Cutov, a two-time European champion who had fought in more than 200 amateur bouts.

But Sugar Ray Leonard, who had been expected to win easily, had a tough time of it. He had injured both hands during his preliminary fights, and the knuckles of his right hand were badly swollen. An injury to the outer edge of his left hand was so severe that he couldn't make a tight fist. Sugar Ray had to endure intense pain in order to defeat Andrés Aldama of Cuba in the light-welterweight finals.

Aldama was a left-hander and a feared puncher, so Leonard kept circling him during their fight and didn't allow the Cuban to get off a single one of his shots. Halfway through the final round, Leonard caught his man squarely with a left hook and followed it with four rights, all to the head. Aldama was out on his feet, and the referee stepped in to stop the fight just as the bell rang. Sugar Ray was awarded a unanimous decision by the boxing judges—and the gold medal.

Charles Mooney won the silver medal in the bantamweight division. He might have won the gold, but he came down with a bad cold before his final fight and lost a decision to a Korean boxer, Yong Jo Gu. And Big John Tate, who was defeated by Cuban Teofilo Stevenson in the semifinals of the heavyweight division, won the bronze medal for third place.

All told, the U.S. boxing team won 35 out of 41 bouts at the '76 Olympics and brought home five gold medals, one silver and one bronze. Not since the 1904 and 1908 Olympics, in which most of the boxers were from either the U.S. or England, had one team so completely dominated the Games. Why did the American boxers do so well? One reason for their success was that they were well coached by Pat Nappi. He realized European–style boxers, including those from Cuba, couldn't fight very effectively when they were backing up, so he told his boxers to keep moving forward. Nappi taught his boxers to avoid their opponents' punches by going from side to side instead of backing up. He also told them to throw lots of jabs followed by combinations of punches. It was a brilliant strategy, and it worked.

After the '76 Olympics, many members of the team went on to become professional boxers. They were just as successful in the pros as they had been as amateurs. John Tate and the Spinks brothers went on to become heavyweight champions, Leo Randolph became super-bantamweight champion, and Sugar Ray Leonard has held many titles, including undisputed middleweight champion and World Boxing Commission light-heavyweight champion.

15

Roger Maris hit his 61st home run on October 1, 1961, breaking Babe Ruth's record of 60 home runs.

BASEBALL

MARIS HITS 61 IN '61:
The 1961 New York
Yankees

A fter the 1960 season when the Yankees lost to the Pittsburgh Pirates in the World Series, New York's long-time manager, Casey Stengel, was fired. He had just turned 70 ("I'll never make that mistake again!" he joked), and Yankees management thought he was too old. Stengel was replaced by Ralph Houk, who was a lot tougher on the players than Stengel had been. Houk ran the team in the same way an Army drill sergeant would run his troops. His instructions to the players were simple: "We have the best team in baseball. Win the 1961 World Championship!"

And that's exactly what they did. But even though the '61 New York Yankees were one of the best teams ever to play the game, they are remembered most for the achievement of just one player. Roger Maris hit 61 home runs that year, breaking Babe Ruth's single-season home run record. It made Maris famous, and in his opinion, fame was the worst thing that ever happened to him.

Maris was the shy, quiet type. He didn't enjoy the national attention he received as he hit home run after home run. Didn't enjoy it? Heck, he *hated* it! From the All-Star break through the end of the season, as he got closer and closer to breaking the record, Maris became a prisoner in the locker room after each game. Reporters from almost every paper in the country crowded around him. He was unable to escape until he answered every single question, and the questions seemed to go on for hours. Many fans didn't want anybody to break the Babe's record, and this made things tougher on Maris. The fans felt that Babe Ruth was the greatest baseball player in history, and Roger Maris—well, Roger Maris couldn't even bat .300.

The Commissioner of Baseball, Ford Frick, also seemed to be against Maris. Early in the season, he pointed out that Ruth had played a 154-game schedule in 1927 when he hit 60 home runs. But Maris would be playing a 162-game season because the American League had extended its season to make room in the schedule for two new teams, the Minnesota Twins and the Los Angeles Dodgers. This gave Maris extra chances to break Ruth's record. Frick ruled that Maris would have to hit his 61st homer in 154 games or fewer; if he did it after that, his record would always have an asterisk next to it in the record books.

Since the Yankees were obviously going to win the American League pennant, Maris's chase for the record gave baseball fans something to get excited about. For a while, it looked as though Maris and his teammate, centerfielder Mickey Mantle (the two were often called "the M&M boys") were *both* going to break Ruth's record. But Mantle slowed down late in the season because of injuries and finished with 54 home runs.

With three games left before the 154-game cutoff, Maris's home run count stood at 58. The Yankees flew into Baltimore for a 4-game series against the Orioles. A crowd of 31,317 showed up for the first two games, a twi-night doubleheader on September 19. When Orioles pitcher Steve Barber walked Maris in the first inning, the spectators booed and hissed. They wanted Maris at least to get a chance to swing the bat. He got his chance, all right, but it didn't do him any good. Barber struck Maris out three times in a row, and the Orioles won the first game 1–0. Maris didn't get a homer in the second game, either.

The next night, September 20, was Maris's last chance to break Ruth's record within the 154-game limit. The ballpark was packed and the press box was overflowing with reporters. Tension rose as Maris stepped up to bat for the first time, but he only lined out to rightfield. Then, in his second at-bat, Maris hit his 59th homer, a 380-foot blast into the rightfield bleachers. The crowd went wild. Only one more home run, and Maris would tie the Babe's record. He almost did, hitting a long fly ball that hooked foul by about 10 feet. Then he struck out. In his last at-bat of the game, Maris grounded out. "I'm glad it's over. The pressure is off," he said afterward.

But it wasn't over and the pressure wasn't off. The Maris-watch continued as intensely as before, even though the cutoff point had come and gone. On September 26, in game 158, the Yankees were playing the Orioles, at home this time. Jack Fisher was on the mound

Whitey Ford beat Babe Ruth's record for pitching consecutive scoreless innings in Game 5 of the 1961 World Series.

for Baltimore when Roger Maris hit his 60th home run. It landed six rows up in the rightfield upper deck as thousands of fans cheered.

Maris didn't hit another homer until the last game of the season. On October 1st, the Yankees were playing the Boston Red Sox at Yankee Stadium. Pitching for Boston was righthander Tracy Stallard. In Maris's second at-bat of the game, he belted one into the rightfield lower deck seats, and the hometown crowd went *crazy*. Roger Maris had broken Babe Ruth's record at last, but he was so shy that he had to be forced to take a bow. After the game, Maris said, "If I never hit another home run, this is one they can never take away from me."

The rest of the team was having a pretty good season that year, too. Yogi Berra, the Yankees catcher throughout the 1950s, had been moved to the outfield because it was easier on his aging legs. Even though Berra was no longer in his prime, he hit 22 home runs. Elston Howard, the team's Number 1 catcher, had a fantastic year, batting .348. Substitute catcher John Blanchard hit 21 home runs in 243 at-bats. The power didn't stop there. Over at first base was Moose Skowron, who hit 28 homers that season. As a team, the Yankees hit 240 home runs in 1961.

Their pitching staff was also excellent. The ace of the staff was future Hall of Famer Whitey Ford, who was having his best year. Ford finished the '61 season with a 25–4 record and a 3.21 ERA.

In the World Series, the Yanks faced the Cincinnati Reds. In the opening game, which was played on October 4 in Yankee Stadium, Elston Howard and Moose Skowron hit solo home runs, but that's all it took, as Ford shut out the Reds 2–0. It was the eighth World Series victory of Whitey Ford's career and set a new record. Cincinnati evened up the series in Game 2 with a 6–2 victory, but the Yanks came back in Game 3, which was played at Cincinnati's Crosley Field. New York won 3–2 on a solo home run by Roger Maris in the ninth inning. In Game 4, Whitey Ford broke another World Series record when he finished pitching his 32nd straight scoreless inning and beat Babe Ruth's record of 29, set in the 1916 and 1918 World Series when Ruth was a pitcher for the Boston Red Sox. Ford had to leave the game at the start of the sixth inning because of an ankle injury, but New York defeated Cincinnati 7–0, then went on to blow the Reds away in Game 5 with a final score of 13–5, winning the championship for a record 19th time. But as the champagne flowed in the Yankees clubhouse, Roger Maris was just relieved that, at last, it was *really* all over.

16

In the 1990 Super Bowl, Joe Montana (center) threw five touchdown passes.

PRO FOOTBALL

DYNASTY ON THE BAY:
The San Francisco 49ers of the 1980s

Have you ever tried to figure out which NFL team was the best ever? If you have, you probably picked the San Francisco 49ers of the 1980s, the 49ers of the present. This team has everything. Their offensive line blocks as well for the run as it does for the pass. The 49ers receivers are among the best in the league. Their defense has been frustrating NFL teams for years. And of course, they have Joe Montana, probably the greatest quarterback of all time.

The 49ers won four Super Bowls in four tries (1982, '85, '89 and '90). This ties the record of the Pittsburgh Steelers, who won four in the 1970s. The 49ers' great performances include individual records as well. Montana holds the record for most Super Bowl passes completed in a career, with 83. Among quarterbacks who have tried at least 40 Super Bowl passes, Montana has completed the most—an amazing 68 percent. He has passed for 1,142 Super Bowl yards, beating the record of the Steelers Terry Bradshaw, who passed for 932, and has thrown an astounding 122 Super Bowl passes *without an interception*. Montana has also thrown 11 Super Bowl touchdown passes, breaking Bradshaw's previous record of 9. And in three out of the 49ers' four Super Bowls, Montana was voted the MVP.

Roger Craig, San Francisco running back, holds the record for most passes caught in Super Bowl play (20). The old record, 16, was held by wide receiver Lynn Swann of the Steelers. And in Super Bowl XXIV, at the end of the 1989–1990 season, Jerry Rice caught his fourth Super Bowl touchdown pass, breaking the previous record of three.

In each of their four Super Bowls, the 49ers haven't allowed their opponents to score more than 21 points. They gave up 21 points to the Cincinnati Bengals in Super Bowl XVI in 1982, 16 points to the Miami Dolphins in Super Bowl XIX, 16 points to the Bengals in Super Bowl XXIII, and 10 points to the Denver Broncos in Super Bowl XXIV.

San Francisco's 55–10 victory over the Broncos was the most one-sided in Super Bowl history. The 49ers had dedicated the game, held in New Orleans on January 28, 1990, to strong safety Jeff Fuller. Earlier in the season, Fuller had suffered an injury to his spine in a game against the New England Patriots. Though he is now improving, no one knows yet whether he will regain the use of his right arm. Running back Roger Craig said, "When he got hurt, we dedicated every game to him. I told him, 'We're gonna get the [Super Bowl] ring for you, buddy. Just enjoy it.' He came into the locker room before the game and that sort of inspired us."

They were inspired, all right! No team had ever scored 55 points in a Super Bowl before. But scoring the most and winning by the biggest margin weren't the only records the 49ers set in the 1990 Super Bowl. Montana's five touchdown passes broke the previous record for touchdown passes in a Super Bowl (4) held by Bradshaw of the Steelers and Doug Williams of the Washington Redskins. Montana also completed 13 passes in a row, breaking the old record of 10, set by Phil Simms of the New York Giants in 1987. Jerry Rice, Montana's favorite pass receiver, caught three touchdown passes, surpassing the

Jerry Rice (foreground) set a record in 1990 by catching his fourth Super Bowl touchdown pass.

old record of two. San Francisco also scored eight touchdowns, which broke the old record of six set by the Redskins in 1988.

In the '90 Super Bowl, the 49ers scored the first time they had the ball. Montana capped a 10-play scoring drive with a 20-yard touchdown pass to Jerry Rice. After Denver made the score 7–3 with a first quarter field goal, the Broncos had the ball for less than one minute out of the next 15. There were only two minutes left in the first half when Broncos quarterback John Elway completed his first pass to a wide receiver. By that time the 49ers had scored three more touchdowns and were ahead 27–3.

By the end of the third quarter, the score was San Francisco 41, Denver 10, and when Montana was finally pulled from the game with 11 minutes left, the 49ers had scored all of their 55 points.

Roger Craig was bursting with joy when he was asked later what he thought of the game Montana had played. "He's like a man from outer space, man," Craig said. "He's like a UFO, man. He knows how to win, Montana. He's like a Green Beret, man!"

A reporter asked Montana, "How about the 49ers, Joe? Are they the best team ever?"

"It would be hard for any team to be better than this team," Montana replied. "You can't play much better than the way the 49ers have this year."

Which is the greatest football team in history? You tell us!

Coach Punch Imlach rebuilt the Toronto Maple Leafs into a powerhouse team that won the Stanley Cup four times in the early '60s.

PRO HOCKEY

THE POWER OF POSITIVE THINKING: The Toronto Maple Leafs of the Late 1950s and Early '60s

When the Toronto Maple Leafs were in last place in the National Hockey League at the end of the 1957–58 season, it looked as if they would *stay* in the cellar for a long time. But they didn't. Instead, they had an amazing turnaround, and it was all due to one man— and he wasn't even a player.

What caused the Leafs to turn around? It was their coach, Punch Imlach. He had a theory: All you had to do to win was believe you were going to win, and it happened just like magic. The Leafs won the Stanley Cup four times in the 1960s.

In most cases, building dynasties is a slow business. That wasn't the case with the Toronto Maple Leafs. They went from being a last-place team to being a contender for the Stanley Cup almost overnight—and all because of positive thinking!

The change began when Punch Imlach was hired as the team's assistant general manager in September 1958, after the Maple Leafs had finished last in the league the previous season. They had a lot of players who didn't play very well and who didn't play very hard either. For two straight years Toronto hadn't made it to the playoffs. Imlach's first task was to get some fresh blood on the team, so he signed Bert Olmstead from the Montreal Canadiens.

Now he needed a goalie. Imlach chose Johnny Bower. Bower was 34 years old and though he had been playing in the minor leagues for many years, he had only one year of NHL experience. It seemed like a gamble, but Imlach didn't think so. He wasn't necessarily trying to get the most talented players in the world. He wanted players with the right attitude—the *winning* attitude.

The Maple Leafs also needed a steady veteran on defense, and Imlach made another move that the "experts" thought was a mistake. He traded a young player named Jim Morrison for veteran Allen Stanley. Though many people thought that Stanley's career was close to being over, he proved Imlach's genius for picking talent by staying with the Maple Leafs for 10 years and being named again and again to the All-Star team.

When the season started, the team didn't seem to be playing any better. By mid-November they had won only 5 of their first 16 games and were still in last place. Imlach knew there was more talent out there on the ice than there had been before, but the team was still not playing hard enough. He decided that this was the fault of the Maple Leafs coach, Billy Reay. So Imlach asked to be promoted to general manager, and the minute he was, he fired Reay and began to coach the team himself.

Though the Leafs lost their first game under Imlach to the Chicago Blackhawks by a score of 2–1, they played well. The next night in Boston, the score was again 2–1, but this time the Leafs came out on top. When the game was over, the team celebrated so wildly you would have thought that they had just won the Stanley Cup.

Imlach continued to get new players for his team, players who thought like winners. He assigned Larry Regan, who had once played for him when he was the coach of the Quebec Aces, to the center position on a line with left wing Dick Duff and right wing George Armstrong. Then Imlach got Gerry Ehman and put him on a line with Billy Harris at center and Frank Mahovlich on left wing.

At last the team began to gel. The chemistry began to feel right, and the Maple Leafs began to win; but by February they were still in the division cellar. Imlach and his team didn't give up. He kept telling his players over and over again that they were going to win the Stanley Cup. The players wanted to believe him, but they knew they had a steep climb if they were going to get one of the four playoff spots by the end of the season.

On March 14, with only four games left in the season, the Maple Leafs were still seven points out of fourth place. Their magic number was *one*: Any combination of *one* New York Rangers win and *one* Maple Leafs loss would mean no trip to the playoffs. Things were made even more exciting because the Leafs and the Rangers were scheduled to play against each other for two games in a row.

To everyone's astonishment, the Maple Leafs won the first game 5–0 and the second 6–5. With two games to go, the Leafs were now only three points out of fourth place. Then the Rangers lost again and the Maple Leafs beat the Montreal Canadiens 6–3. The Leafs' magic number was still *one*: They were only *one* point away from a playoff spot with *one* game left to go.

The final game of the season was against the Detroit Red Wings in Detroit. The Maple Leafs quickly fell behind in the first period, 2–0. Then the scoreboard lit up: MONTREAL 4, NEW YORK 2, FINAL. The Rangers had lost! All the Leafs had to do was win this *one* game and they would be in the playoffs.

That was all the inspiration they needed. The Maple Leafs won the game 6–4, and the team that the experts had predicted would finish in last place had made the playoffs. Some people thought it was a miracle, but not Punch Imlach. He knew it was simply a matter of positive thinking.

The Maple Leafs kept on winning. In the semifinals of the playoffs, they faced the Boston Bruins in a best-of-seven series. The teams were so evenly matched that they had to play all seven games, but it was the Maple Leafs who won the all-important seventh game. That put them into the Stanley Cup finals against the Montreal Canadiens.

Though the Leafs played hard, Montreal won. The loss of the Stanley Cup didn't discourage Imlach. His positive thinking went on and on, and the Maple Leafs got better and better. By the 1960–61 season, they were the best hockey team in the NHL. In Imlach's third year as their coach, they finally won the Stanley Cup. During the '60s, they presented the trophy to Imlach four times. In 1962, the Leafs defeated the Chicago Blackhawks in six games, and in 1963 they beat the Detroit Red Wings in five. But it took the full seven games for the Leafs to beat the Red Wings in 1964.

Punch Imlach's positive thinking influenced many of his players for life. One member of the team, defenseman Al Arbour, went on to become part of another NHL dynasty as coach of the New York Islanders, who won four Stanley Cups in the early '80s.

18

The 1960 U.S. Olympic basketball team. Labels: Lucas, Holderson, Boozer, Dischinger, Robertson, A. Kelly, Smith, Arnette, West, Dean Nesmith Trainer, Lane, Warren Womble Ass't. Coach, Dutch Lonborg Mgr., Pete Newell Coach, 1st Pl...

The 1960 U.S. Olympic basketball team would have been one of the best professional teams of all time had they continued to play together after the Rome Olympics.

OLYMPIC BASKETBALL

WINNING THE GOLD WITHOUT BREAKING A SWEAT: The 1960 U.S. Team

I f the U.S. basketball team had stayed together after the 1960 Olympics in Rome, Italy, it might have been the greatest professional team of all time. The team had future pro stars like Jerry West, Oscar Robertson, Jerry Lucas and Walt Bellamy. The team was so strong that future Boston Celtics great

John Havlicek qualified only as an alternate, which meant he was first in line to replace a player who had to drop out.

Four members of that team went on to win the NBA Rookie of the Year Award: Robertson in 1960–61, Bellamy in 1961–62, Dischinger in 1962–63 and Lucas in 1963–64. In their NBA careers, Bellamy and Lucas each pulled down more than 12,000 rebounds. Robertson and West are among the all-time NBA leaders in assists, and between them they made passes leading to a score more than 16,000 times. West, Bellamy and Robertson each played 14 NBA seasons and each scored more than 20,000 points.

The 1960 U.S. team's coach was Pete Newell, whose regular job then was coaching basketball at the University of California at Berkeley. In spite of the awesome individual talents of his players, Newell didn't take it for granted that they would win. He knew he had to teach his men how to play as a *team* because teamwork is the key to winning championships. Newell's players all came from different colleges, and he had only a few weeks in August, 1960 to turn the 12 terrific players into one terrific team.

Though most teams that Newell had coached were known for their slow, controlled style of basketball, he decided not to use that strategy with the Olympic team. "It would have been like trying to hold back a fast car," he said. "Even though it wasn't my style, I knew the fast break was *their* style."

Newell organized his team's offense loosely, giving the players the freedom to decide how to move the ball and score. But there was nothing loose about the team's defense. Newell gave strict lessons on defense so that the U.S. team would be the best in the world at both ends of the court. He also insisted that the players keep themselves in top physical condition.

"I was in the best shape of my life going into the Olympics," said Jerry West.

Soon it was clear that this team would be very special. "Until that time, there had never been a team as good as us," Terry Dischinger said.

West added, "It was a very powerful team. As the tournament went on, the team continued to grow. I had a wonderful experience playing on the team and for a great coach."

The U.S. played its first Olympic game against the Italian team on August 26 in the Little Sports Palace in Rome. When the Italian team scored the first basket, the crowd cheered so loudly that the roof shook. But that was about the last thing the Italian fans could cheer for. By halftime the U.S. led 42–17, and the score never got any closer in the second half. In its second game the U.S. team played Japan, but the Japanese players were too short to present much of a challenge—the tallest man on Japan's team was 6'2", while the average height of the U.S. starting five was 6'7". The final score was U.S. 126, Japan 42.

The U.S. defeated Hungary 107–67 in its third game, then went on to blow out Yugoslavia 104–42 and Uruguay 108–80. Against Hungary, five American players scored in double figures. Against Uruguay, six of them did it. In that game, Adrian Smith led the U.S. team with 15 points, Robertson and Bellamy had 13 each, West scored 11, Dischinger scored 10 and Burdette Haldorson came off the bench to score 10 points as well.

There are several reasons for the U.S. team's fantastic performance in the 1960 Olympics. For one thing, the players were all exceptionally talented. For another, they were often playing against men who were a lot shorter than they were. And then there were the balls used in the Olympics. The balls were not very good; they were made of very smooth, untextured leather and were very slippery. This made them harder to shoot accurately from long distances. Rather than taking their chances with long shots, the Americans decided to shoot everything from close range, and more of their shots went in.

After the U.S. team defeated Uruguay, it had to face the team from the Soviet Union. This game wasn't going to be as easy to win as the others had been. The Soviet team had the only players in the tournament who were taller than the Americans. At the end of the first half, the U.S. was ahead 35–28, but it had been a battle all the way. The Soviets were playing rough, but the referees weren't calling many fouls against them. That made the Americans mad. Oscar Robertson was warned twice about outbursts of temper. In the second half, Robertson scored 12 points, which made his total for the game 14, and the U.S. won 81–57. West led the team by scoring 19 points and Lucas added 16.

The U.S. team next played Italy again in the Olympic semifinals. This game was even rougher than the one against the Soviet Union—the teams were called for a total of 71 fouls! The Italians' star player, Gianfranco Lombardi, scored 25 points, the most that any player had scored against the U.S., but it wasn't enough. All five U.S. starters scored in double figures, and the final score was United States 112, Italy 81.

The U.S. team played for the gold medal against Brazil on September 10. The Brazilians played hard, but they were no match for the Americans. Center Jerry Lucas scored repeatedly on many layups and tip-ins from under his own basket. By the end of the first half, he had scored 18 points. The score at halftime was U.S. 50, Brazil 24. In the second half, the U.S. team used players from its bench and cruised easily to a 27-point victory. Final score: United States 90, Brazil 63.

Lucas was the game's high scorer with 25 points, Robertson scored 12, Dischinger made 11, Lane scored 9 and West scored 6 points during the contest. The high scorer for the Brazilians was Walmir Marques, with 18 points.

No one was surprised that the Americans won the gold. It had seemed all along that victory was their destiny, and now that destiny had been fulfilled.

CHAPTER 19

Golfers like Seve Ballesteros of Spain helped Europe win back the Ryder Cup in 1985.

GOLF

A SHIFT OF POWER: The European Ryder Cup Teams of the 1980s

The Ryder Cup is a tournament that pits a team of the 12 best golfers from the United States against the 12 best from countries in Europe. They play a series of singles and pairs competitions, and the team that wins the most matches wins the Cup. The tournament is held every two years and takes place over a three-day period.

For 60 years, the United States had almost always won the Ryder Cup, but that domination came to an end in the 1980s, when a new breed of European golfer came on the scene. Players like Seve (SEH-VEE) Ballesteros of Spain, Bernhard Langer of West Germany, Nick Faldo of England, Ian Woosnam of Wales and Sandy Lyle of Scotland are among the best golfers in the world.

The Europeans first took the Ryder Cup from the Americans in 1985 on a course near Birmingham, England. The U.S. golfers were humiliated because they felt they had lost the Cup to a team that wasn't as good as they were. But in 1987, the Europeans did it again, proving that their victory in '85 hadn't been just a fluke. They really *did* have the better team. Their coach was Tony Jacklin of England, and he encouraged them to play aggressive golf, to risk disaster in order to make great shots rather than playing it safe as the U.S. team tended to do.

In '87, the tournament was held at the Muirfield Village Golf Club in Dublin, Ohio. Amazingly enough, 1,500 golf fans from Europe had crossed the Atlantic to watch the matches. Though the rest of the gallery of fans was made up of Americans—20,000 of them—the Europeans were the loudest and most enthusiastic.

Ballesteros was the best player in this tournament, astounding the spectators again and again with his wonderful shots. It seemed that the more pressure he was under, the better he played. Ballesteros thought that it was the European fans in the crowd that made him play so well. "When you play for so many, you get strong," he said.

Of the 12 singles matches in the '87 Ryder Cup, 8 of them were decided on the 18th and final hole. Of those eight, the Americans lost three and tied five. On the 18th hole of his match against England's Howard Clark, U.S. golfer Dan Pohl had a lot of trouble getting his ball out of a sand trap, and ended up losing by one stroke. Larry Mize of the U.S. was one stroke ahead of his opponent, Sam Torrance of Scotland, going into the 18th hole, when Mize hooked his tee shot into the creek that runs along the right side of the fairway. The match ended in a tie.

Against Eamonn Darcy of Ireland, Ben Crenshaw of the U.S. was putting with his one-iron because he had broken his putter after three-putting the green on the sixth hole. When someone suggested later that he had broken his putter because he was so mad at himself, Crenshaw denied it. "I just tapped it down on a walnut, and it snapped," he said.

Going into the final hole, the match between Crenshaw and Darcy was close. Darcy drove first, and hit his ball very far, right down the center fairway. He couldn't have driven better. But Crenshaw hooked his shot just the same way Mize had done—and his ball landed in that exact same creek. Naturally, Darcy ended up winning the match.

The Europeans' Ryder Cup victory was assured when Ballesteros shot three under par to defeat Curtis Strange in their singles match. After the tournament was over, European coach Jacklin said, "I never thought I'd live to see golf played like it was today. *Incredible* is not enough to say."

Golfing great Jack Nicklaus, the coach of the American team, admitted that the Europeans had played better under pressure. "The 18th hole was the difference," he said. "That's where I would have expected our guys to win, but our guys weren't quite as tough as the Europeans."

In 1989, the Europeans almost did it again—almost, but not quite. Again Seve Ballesteros was the best golfer on the team. During his doubles match with teammate José-Maria Olazabal against the U.S. team of Tom Watson and Mark O'Meara, Ballesteros had one stretch on the back nine (holes 10-18) when he went eagle (two strokes under par for one hole), birdie (one stroke under par), birdie, birdie, birdie. That's five strokes under par for four holes. That's hot!

In the doubles match that pitted Sam Torrance and Gordon Brand, Jr. of Europe against Curtis Strange and Paul Azinger of the U.S., the pairs were tied going into the final hole. Both Europeans bogeyed (went one over par) on the 18th hole. Then Azinger won the hole and the match with a difficult par that included a great shot out of a sand trap next to the green.

When all the '89 matches had been completed and the final score showed that the teams were tied, 14–14, Tony Jacklin commented, "It was a fair result. The Americans were bloody tough. And determined. And so are we. That's the fun of it. It's been a wonderful feast of golf!"

Since the Americans had won the tournament so many times in the past, the tie made the Europeans very proud. Besides, since they had won the Cup in 1987, the tie meant they got to keep it for another two years.

20

Lyudmila Tourischeva was the best gymnast on the 1976 Soviet women's Olympic team.

OLYMPIC GYMNASTICS

PERFECT BALANCE: The 1976 Soviet Women's Team

Everyone remembers that 14-year-old Nadia Comaneci of Romania was the first gymnast to score two perfect 10s in the same Olympics. She earned those amazing scores in 1976 for her performance on the uneven parallel bars and the balance beam. Comaneci was the best individual gymnast in the world at that time, but it's important to realize that in the same year, the Soviet Union had probably the best women's gymnastic *team* in the world. And though she didn't get nearly as much publicity as Comaneci (co-man-EETCH), Soviet gymnast Nelli Kim also earned two perfect 10s in the '76 Olympics.

In addition to Kim, the Soviet team featured Lyudmila Tourishcheva (toor-IS-chay-vuh), who came in third in the all-around competition behind Comaneci and Kim; and Olga Korbut, who had been as popular at the '72 Olympics as Comaneci was in '76. The 1972 Olympics were held in Munich, Germany, and because Korbut was so little and cute, the newspapers started calling her "the Munchkin of Munich."

In 1976, Tourishcheva was the best gymnast on the Soviet team, but she never became as famous as either Korbut or Comaneci, who stole the spotlight because, like Korbut, she captured the imagination of the public. Women's gymnastics is a sport for the very young and the very small, and Lyudmila was both older and taller than Korbut and the other members of the Soviet team. Actually, she was only 5'4¹/₂", but compared to her 15-year-old teammate, Maria Filatova, she seemed big and tough. Filatova was 4'3³/₄" tall and weighed only 66 pounds. Filatova sometimes sat on Tourishcheva's lap between performances, and when the press asked Filatova what she liked to do when she wasn't practicing gymnastics, she said in a high squeaky voice, "I read my books, I go to the movies, I play with my dolls."

Between the '72 and '76 Olympics, the Soviet team had toured the United States. Thousands turned out to see Olga Korbut, but nobody paid much attention to Tourishcheva or the other members of the team. Korbut wasn't very popular with her teammates, particularly Tourishcheva, who didn't like being upstaged by a gymnast who wasn't as good as she was. And it didn't make Lyudmila any happier when, just a few days before the '76 Games began, she was replaced by Olga as the captain of the Soviet team by the Soviet Training Council because they wanted cute little Olga to carry the flag during the opening ceremonies!

But when the competition began, what mattered to all of the Soviet gymnasts was doing the best they could for the honor of their country. Both Korbut and Tourishcheva performed well, but this time the Romanian, Nadia Comaneci, was constantly in the spotlight. And after Comaneci won the first 10 ever awarded in Olympic gymnastics, for her performance on the uneven parallel bars, the Soviet coaches got angry. They said it was impossible to score a 10 because that meant perfection, and *nobody,* was perfect. When Nelli Kim earned a 10 in the side horse vault; however, they didn't complain at all.

Kim won her two gold medals in the vault and the floor exercise, in which she also earned a perfect 10. Tourishcheva came in second in the floor exercise to bring home the silver, and Comaneci won the bronze. In the vault, Tourishcheva tied for second place with Carola Dombeck from East Germany. Comaneci's perfect score in the balance beam competition earned the gold, Korbut won the silver and Tourishcheva finished fourth.

Every member of the Soviet team finished in the top 10 overall. They won the Team Combined gold medal, scoring a total of 466 points. Nelli Kim and Tourishcheva tied for the team lead, with 78.25 points each. Olga Korbut finished third on the team and fifth overall; Elvira Saadi finished seventh overall, and Filatova and Svetlana

Soviet gymnast Olga Korbut captured the attention of the press in 1976 because she was so little and so cute.

Grozdova (groz-DOE-va) tied for ninth place overall. Tourishcheva's four medals in 1976 brought her total for the '72 and '76 Olympics to four gold medals, two silver and three bronze. Lyudmila may not have been the star of the tournament, but she and the other members of the Soviet team proved that you don't have to be constantly in the spotlight to be the best.

21

Leo Durocher (left) of the 1934 St. Louis Cardinals was called "The Lip" because he loved to yell at umpires.

BASEBALL

THE GASHOUSE GANG:
The 1934 St. Louis Cardinals

In the midst of America's Great Depression in the 1930s, here was a group of mangy ballplayers everybody could identify with. The St. Louis Cardinals, otherwise known as The Gashouse Gang, were made up of ex-coal miners and cotton-pickers. They scrapped their way to a world championship with Leo (The Lip)

Durocher at shortstop and two pitchers called Dizzy and Daffy Dean.

The Dean brothers were known for their pranks. Jay (Dizzy) Dean once put a chunk of ice on home plate. How come? "To cool off my fast ball," Dizzy said. His lifetime record was 150–83, good enough to get into the Hall of Fame. In 1934, Dizzy was at his best. Before the season started, he bragged that he and his brother Paul were going to win 45 games combined that year. He was wrong. They won 49!

The '34 Cards loved to yell at umpires. Leo Durocher and manager/second baseman Frankie Frisch were the worst—and the loudest. They cursed so often that the umpires began to call the close ones against the Cards. Frisch was called "The Fordham Flash" because he was a graduate of Fordham University in the Bronx, a borough of New York City. In 1934, he was in his first year of being both a manager and a player. Not only did he manage his team to a world championship but he also batted .305.

Throwing water balloons was the hobby of Cardinals first baseman Ripper Collins, who led the National League in homers with 35. The third baseman was Pepper Martin. His trademark was his dirty uniform. He liked to slide head first, which was much less common then than it is now. In 1934, Martin batted .289 and led the National League in stolen bases. Another star on the team was leftfielder Joe Medwick, one of the best hitters in the history of the game. His lifetime batting average was .324.

The Cardinals centerfielder was Ernie Orsatti, who moonlighted during the off-season in Hollywood, working as a movie stuntman. The rightfielder was Jack Rothrock, the only Cardinal besides Ripper Collins who appeared in every game that year. The team's catching duties were split between Virgil (Spud) Davis and Bill Delancey, who batted over .300 for the year.

The Cards had not always been winners. In 1933, they had finished fifth in the league, and at the start of the '34 season they lost 7 of their first 11 games. By Labor Day, with one month left in the season, they were seven games behind the first-place New York Giants.

On September 13, the Cardinals traveled to New York's Polo Grounds to play the Giants in a four-game series. If the Cards won, they were back in the pennant race. If they lost, they were history. Daffy Dean pitched an 11-inning shutout in the first game to beat the Giants 2–0. New York won the second game 4–1, but the Dean brothers pitched both ends of a doubleheader the next day and swept the Giants. The Cardinals were still in the race.

On September 21, the Cards played another doubleheader, this time against the Brooklyn Dodgers at Ebbets Field. Dizzy pitched a three-hitter in the first game and Daffy pitched a no-hitter in the second. After the games were over, Dizzy told the press, "If I'da knowed Paul

Cardinals pitcher Jay (Dizzy) Dean kept the fans amused by his outrageous antics.

was gonna pitch a no-hitter, I'da pitched one, too!"

The Cardinals went on to sweep the Cincinnati Reds 4–0, 6–1, 9–0 and win the pennant. In the World Series they played the Detroit Tigers. The Tigers infield committed five errors in Game 1 and Dizzy beat them 8–3. Detroit evened up the series when "Schoolboy" Rowe, the Tigers best pitcher, defeated the Cards 3–2 in a game that went 12 innings. In Game 3, Daffy Dean beat Detroit 4–1, but the Tigers tied the series up again in the fourth game, beating the Cardinals 10–4.

Even though Dizzy Dean did not pitch in that game, he still made the headlines. He was sent in late in the game as a pinch-runner and was running from first to second base when the second baseman's relay throw hit him right between the eyes. Dean had to be carried off the field and taken to the hospital where he was x-rayed to make sure he didn't have a fractured skull. "They x-rayed my head and found nothin'," Dizzy said to the press. If he knew that what he was saying was funny, he didn't let on.

Dean had a headache the next day, but it wasn't bad enough to keep him from being the starting pitcher in Game 5. It might have made a difference, though, because the Tigers beat the Cards 3–1. To win the championship, the Cardinals had to win the last two games of the series. Both games were played in Detroit.

Daffy Dean started for St. Louis in Game 6. In the seventh inning, Durocher hit a double to knock in the winning run. Final score: Cards 4, Tigers 3.

In the final game, Dizzy returned to the mound for the Cardinals. St. Louis busted the game wide open in the third inning, scoring seven runs. In the sixth inning, Joe Medwick slid hard into Tigers third baseman Marv Owen with his spikes high. This is considered unsportsmanlike, and Medwick and Owen began swinging at each other. The umps broke up the fight, but when Medwick tried to take his position in leftfield the next inning, the Detroit fans pelted him with garbage. Finally Judge Kenesaw Mountain Landis, the Commissioner of Baseball, ordered Medwick out of the game for his own protection and so the game could continue.

With Dizzy still on the mound, the Cards were ahead 11–0 going into the ninth inning. Dean began to goof around, laughing at the Tigers hitters who had swung and missed. On the last pitch of the game, which was to Hank Greenberg, Dean turned his back on the plate before the ball arrived. Greenberg swung–and missed. The Gashouse Gang had become the most unlikely champions in baseball history!

22

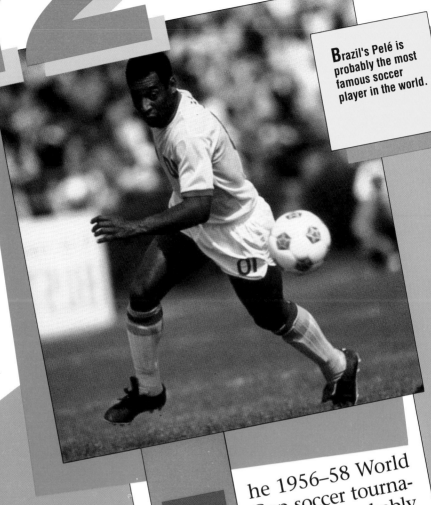

Brazil's Pelé is probably the most famous soccer player in the world.

SOCCER

BRAZIL'S THE BEST:
Brazilian National
Team, Winners of
the 1958 World Cup

The 1956–58 World Cup soccer tournament was probably the longest single tournament in sports history. It began late in 1956 when Austria beat Luxembourg in Vienna 7–0, and finished in mid-1958. Fifty-three teams competed at the beginning and by the end only two teams were left—Brazil and

Sweden. It also had the biggest audience of any soccer tournament up until that time. Soccer games had begun to be televised in 1954, so people all over the world were able to watch the World Cup.

During this tournament, the Brazilian players changed the face of soccer (or football, as it is known everywhere except the United States). They did it by placing four men in attacking position in what is called the 4-2-4 formation. Before that, most teams had played a 3-2-1-4 formation, which made for a more conservative game. Brazil didn't have to worry as much about defense as other teams did. And Brazil had a secret weapon, a 17-year-old inside forward named Edson Arantes do Nascimento and called simply "Pelé" (PAY-lay). Nobody had ever heard of him before, but he was soon to become the greatest soccer player in the world.

The final 16 teams of the original 53 played their games in Rasunda Stadium in Stockholm, Sweden. Sweden was soccer-crazy during the tournament and the Swedish team was one of the favorites to win. The Brazilian team was the other. Life had not been easy for the Brazilians since their arrival in Stockholm. The Swedish fans had not treated them very well. The Brazilian players were heckled on the street, though players from other teams were admired and respected. You see, the Swedish fans knew that the Brazilians were good. They just didn't know *how* good.

Brazil's toughest game in the final rounds came against England. The teams played to a scoreless tie. English goalie Colin MacDonald deserved a lot of credit for preventing such a powerful team from scoring. Wales also gave Brazil a hard time. There was no score until late in the game when Pelé rifled a shot past the Welsh goalie for the win. In their game against the Soviet Union, the Brazilians won easily 2–0. Amazingly, Brazil entered the semifinals of the tournament without being scored on. But that ended with the semifinal game against France.

The stadium was packed for that game. At one point Brazilian Manoel (Garrincha) dos Santos, who was playing outside right, nudged the ball gently with his toe. When a French defender charged him, Garrincha threw a head fake one way and went the other way. That left his defender dazed and confused, as well as out of the play.

Garrincha made a centering pass, received a return pass and shot a rocket off his instep toward the goal. Even though the shot missed by inches, the crowd cheered. They were enjoying the show. They were also beginning to wonder if Sweden would be able to beat Brazil in the finals.

France became the first team to score against Brazil's airtight defense, but it was not enough. Using expert passes, light-footed dribbling and scoring shots that looked as if they came from a cannon, Brazil defeated France 5–2. Pelé scored three goals in the second half.

When Sweden met Brazil in the finals, there was no doubt in anyone's mind that this would be a match between the two best soccer teams in the world. The teams had very different images. The Brazilians were known for their finesse. They had turned soccer into an art. The Swedes, on the other hand, had a reputation for being the the roughest, toughest team in Europe. They'd just as soon knock you down as look at you.

In Brazil, everything ground to a halt so that everyone could listen to the radio broadcast of the game. Those who didn't have radios or television sets gathered in the public squares where the radio broadcast was amplified through loudspeakers. The president of Brazil even postponed an important political conference until the game was over.

Sweden was convinced that the Brazilians would panic and give up if they fell behind. So the Swedes decided they had to score first, and they did. Nils Liedholm's goal four minutes into the first half put the Swedes ahead 1–0.

But Sweden's plan didn't work. Brazil *didn't* panic and they *didn't* quit. They played harder than ever. At halftime the Brazilians were ahead 2–1. In the second half, Pelé was truly awesome. He took a crossing pass, bounced the ball off his thigh high over a defender, ran around the man and caught the ball on his thigh again before shooting the ball into the net for a goal. It was a spectacular play that is still talked about today, and it put his team ahead 3–1.

The Swedes continued to play hard but they never had a chance against Pelé and the Brazilians. Brazil won the championship 5–2. Pelé scored the last goal of the game. It was a header, which means that he hit the ball into the goal with his head.

When the Brazilians returned home, they were welcomed like conquering heroes. But the star of the tournament was Pelé, the kid with only one name. A legend had begun.

23

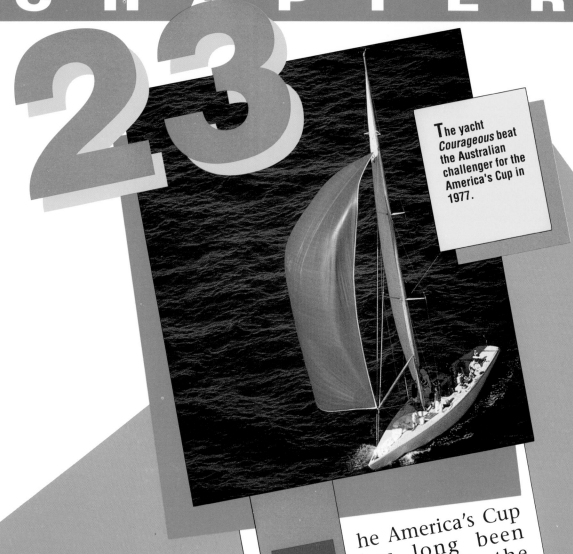

The yacht *Courageous* beat the Australian challenger for the America's Cup in 1977.

YACHTING

CAPTAIN
OUTRAGEOUS AND
HIS CREW:
Ted Turner's
Successful 1977
Defense of the
America's Cup

The America's Cup has long been considered the most prestigious prize in international yacht racing. This is despite the fact that the U.S. overcame challenge after challenge from other countries and held on to the Cup for more than a century.

The New York Yacht Club

(NYYC) first won the Cup in 1851 when the yacht *America* beat the best of England's Royal Yacht Squadron in British waters. The NYYC still had the cup in 1977. By that time, the racers all used the same type of boat called 12-Meters, although they are not actually 12 meters long. They are called that because of an obscure hull measurement that even the sailors don't understand very well.

Each America's Cup competition is divided into three parts. First there are races to determine which boat will defend the Cup for the host country. Then there are races to determine which foreign boat has the right to challenge for the Cup. Finally the two boats selected race in a best-of-seven series (the first boat to win four races gets the Cup).

In 1977 the yacht selected to challenge for the Cup was *Australia*, which was both the best foreign boat and the best Australian boat. *Australia* represented the Sun City Yacht Club in Perth, Australia.

Defending the Cup for the NYYC was *Courageous,* skippered by millionaire Ted Turner, an entrepreneur in the communications business. He won the honor to defend by defeating *Enterprise,* with respected sailmaker Lowell North at the helm.

Turner's aggressive personality had caused trouble right from the start of his involvement in yacht racing. He is probably the only skipper to defend the America's Cup who was twice turned down for membership in the NYYC before finally being allowed in. But if Turner was unpopular with the old-timers in yachting circles, the opposite was true of his relationship with the press. Newspaper and television reporters followed Turner wherever he went. Whatever he did was news. Before the start of the first race in 1977, Turner directed *Courageous* to pass very close to the press boat so he could tip his cap for the cameras. His flamboyant style earned the sport of yacht racing the kind of publicity it had never had before, and won Turner himself a spot on the cover of *Sports Illustrated.*

Turner's crew on *Courageous* had been together for several years before they raced in '77. They had raced Turner's boat *Tenacious* before the America's Cup races and between Cup campaigns, and three-quarters of them had been with him aboard *Mariner* in 1974 when Turner had first tried to defend the Cup. *Mariner* hadn't done well that year and was not chosen to represent the club. Now, three years later, Turner and his crew had a chance to prove that they had learned from their experience. Lesson Number One: Get a better boat.

Veteran crew member Marty O'Meara explained, "[On *Mariner*] we were good sailors on a dog of a boat. We were desperate for a chance to prove how good we were on a *good* boat."

It's unusual for a skipper who has been defeated in a previous competition to try again, but then Ted Turner was—and is—a very unusual man. Though he often yelled at his crew, they were fiercely loyal to him. According to one source, Turner had them believing he was the reincarnation of Vince Lombardi. (See Chapter 27.)

Turner's right-hand man aboard *Courageous* was the tactician, Gary Jobson. It was Jobson's task to plot the course for the boat, taking into consideration the wind shifts and the position of the competition. He came up with the racing strategies. Many people think it was Jobson's quick thinking that led to *Courageous's* complete domination over the Australian yacht, but Jobson admitted that Turner didn't always accept his advice. Captain Outrageous sometimes followed his own instincts, even though facts and figures told him to do something else.

The teams that compete in the America's Cup do not consist of just the captain and his crew, however. Also included are the boat's owner, her builder and her designer. They all deserve equal credit for any victory. *Courageous* was owned by the Kings Point Merchant Marine

The crew of *Courageous.* (Left to right, bottom row) Dick Sadler, Bunky Helfrich, Robbie Doyle, Stretch Ryder. (Left to right, top row) John Edgecomb, Captain Ted Turner, Gary Jobson, Con Findley, Paul Fuchs, Bill Jorch, Max O'Meara, Richie Boyd. (Missing from picture: Richard Collins.)

Academy. She had been designed by the firm of Sparkman and Stephens, and built at a boatyard called Minneford's. This same team of designers and builders had been producing winning yachts for the NYYC since 1964.

Courageous held off the Australian challenge in 1977 by beating the boat from "Down Under" in four straight races in the waters off Newport, Rhode Island. (The NYYC is based in New York City so its home waters are two rivers. Newport is located on the Atlantic, which is much better for yacht racing.) With the exception of the very beginning of the first race, held on September 13, *Australia* was never ahead. Even though *Australia* got to the starting line 16 seconds ahead of *Courageous,* the American yacht was actually in better position with respect to the wind. This was clear at the first mark, where *Courageous* was ahead by 1 minute and 8 seconds. *Courageous* would never be behind again, and won by 1 minute and 48 seconds.

The second race, held three days later, was by far the closest. *Courageous* and *Australia* were side by side right until the final leg of the race, when the American boat reacted better to a slight shift in the wind. The victory was by 1 minute, 3 seconds. In the third race, *Courageous* beat *Australia* by 2 minutes and 32 seconds, and her fourth and final victory was by 2 minutes and 25 seconds.

At the press conference after his victory, Turner and his crew (Jobson, Richard Boyd, Robbie Doyle, John Edgecomb, Con Findley, Bunky Helfrich, Bill Jorch, O'Meara, Stretch Ryder, Dick Sadler Richard Collins and Paul Fuchs) fielded questions from the reporters. Turner, as usual, did most of the talking.

"I never raced against such good sportsmen as my friends from Australia," he said. "I love the Australians. I love everybody in this room."

When Turner had finished talking to the reporters, he was lifted up onto the shoulders of his crew and carried from the building. It wasn't a press conference anymore—it was a celebration!

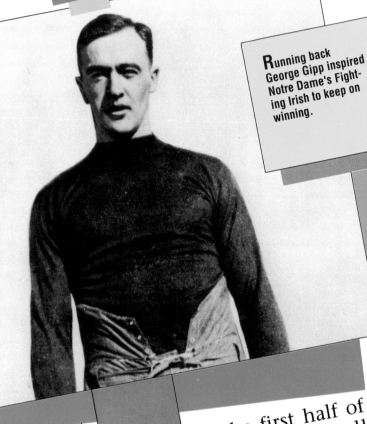

CHAPTER 24

Running back George Gipp inspired Notre Dame's Fighting Irish to keep on winning.

COLLEGE FOOTBALL

WINNING FOR THE GIPPER: Knute Rockne's Fighting Irish of Notre Dame

For the first half of the 1920 football season, running back George Gipp of Notre Dame was the greatest. Averaging 113.5 yards per game of total offense, Gipp guided the Fighting Irish of Notre Dame to an undefeated season and recognition as the best college team in the nation. But Gipp was not there to celebrate with his teammates. He got sick during the season and on December 14, 1920, he died.

His last words, whispered to his coach, Knute Rockne, became famous. They were an inspiration to his teammates, and to all future Notre Dame football players: "When things are wrong and the breaks are beating the boys, tell them to give it all they've got and win one just for the Gipper."

Knute Rockne's most famous football team was the 1925 squad. This was the team of the "Four Horsemen of the Apocalypse," a name given to Notre Dame's offensive backfield—the quarterback, two halfbacks and a fullback. The name came about when Notre Dame played against Army. It was the first time these two football greats had ever faced each other. The game was played at the Polo Grounds in New York, a neutral site. Rockne was always trying to come up with something new to confuse the opposition, and that year it was his backfield shift. Just before the snap of the ball, the four players that made up Notre Dame's offensive backfield would all shift their positions at the same time. Because of the shift, the defense didn't know where the running backs were going to line up until almost the very instant the ball was snapped.

During the game against Army, George Strickler, Notre Dame's publicity director, watched the shift again and again from the press box. "They look like the Four Horsemen of the Apocalypse," he said, referring to the latest silent film starring Rudolph Valentino. Newspaper columnist Grantland Rice overheard Strickler's comment and repeated it in the newspaper. Immediately those four players (Stuhldreher, Miller, Crowley and Layden) became known as The Four Horsemen. The next morning, Strickler had a photo taken of the Irish backfield—on horseback. That photo is one of the most famous football photographs of all time, and Notre Dame's Four Horsemen remain the most famous backfield in football history, college or pro.

Inspired by the memory of the Gipper, coach Rockne's team continued winning games. Rockne believed in playing his entire team, and giving every player an important role. The Four Horsemen were known for their terrific speed. In a flash, they'd be through any hole in the defense and down the field. But they rarely started a game. Rockne correctly figured that the Four Horsemen would do even better when they were playing against a defense that was slightly tired. So he started each game with his so-called Shock Troops. These were the heaviest (and probably the slowest) players on the fighting Irish team. Their job was to put as much wear and tear on the other team's defense as possible until Coach Rockne sent in the Horsemen. The Shock Troops usually started the second half, too, so they could wear down the defense once again.

This 1925 photograph of Notre Dame's backfield on horseback is one of the most famous football photos of all time.

The combination of the Shock Troops and the Horsemen was so successful that Notre Dame finished the 1925 season undefeated and won the national championship.

Because they were so exciting to watch, the Fighting Irish became the most popular team in the country as well as the best. Notre Dame played in the Rose Bowl on New Year's Day, 1926. The opposing team was from Stanford University and it, too, was undefeated that season. Stanford was coached by "Pop" Warner, whose name remains famous today because a national junior football program is named after him. The game between Notre Dame and Stanford helped make the Rose Bowl the major sporting event it is today.

After Notre Dame's Shock Troops took the field for a couple of drives and failed to score, the Four Horsemen entered the game. The flashy backfield fumbled the ball on its first possession and Stanford recovered it. Stanford got on the scoreboard with a 17-yard field goal by Murray Cuddeback. Several plays later, Notre Dame's Elmer Layden ran the ball into the end zone; but the Fighting Irish missed with the kick for the extra point, and the score was Notre Dame 6, Stanford 3.

Stanford got the ball back, but Layden intercepted a pass thrown by Stanford fullback Ernie Nevers and returned it all the way for his second touchdown of the game.

In the second half, Notre Dame scored another touchdown, but so did Stanford, cutting the Irish lead to 20–10. In the fourth quarter, Stanford ran five straight successful plays. They drove the ball to the Irish 1-yard line. There the Stanford attack ground to a halt. Four times there was a loud crash on the line of scrimmage as the Irish put up a stunning goal-line stand.

Before the game was over, Elmer Layden picked off yet another Nevers pass and returned the interception 70 yards for the final score of the game. The Irish had won the Rose Bowl 27–10.

Pop Warner was furious. He thought his team had outplayed Notre Dame for most of the game. The Stanford offense had gained almost 300 yards while the Irish offense had gained only 179. But points, not yards gained, win football games. The Irish had something else working in their favor—motivation.

Chalk up another one for the Gipper!

25

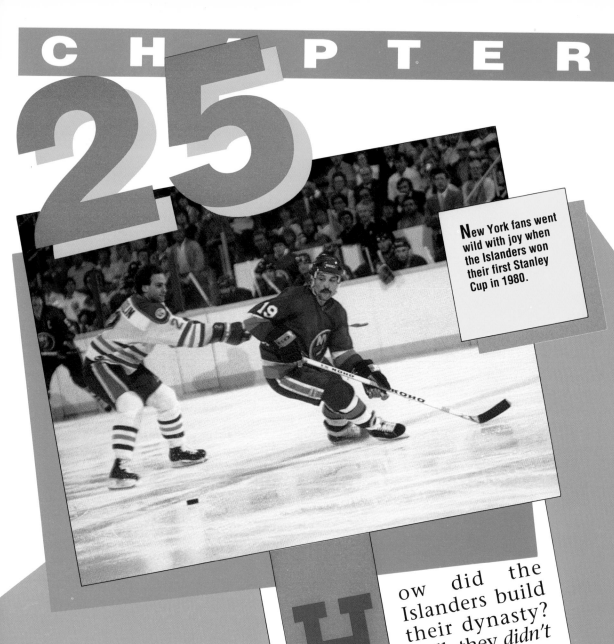

New York fans went wild with joy when the Islanders won their first Stanley Cup in 1980.

PRO HOCKEY

A DYNASTY COMES TO LONG ISLAND: The 1980–83 New York Islanders

How did the Islanders build their dynasty? Well, they *didn't* do it by trading for superstars the way many other teams did. Instead, they did it with a combination of scouting and recruiting. The scouts scoured small Canadian towns and the junior hockey leagues. The Islanders top-notch scouting and recruiting system was the idea of Bill Torrey, the general manager.

"Sure, everybody has scouts," Torrey says. "Ours are just better."

Their scouting turned up three NHL Rookies-of-the-Year in five years. They were defenseman Denis Potvin in 1974, center Bryan Trottier (trot-YAY) in 1976 and right wing Mike Bossy in 1978.

Another reason the Islanders were so successful was their coach, Al Arbour. Arbour had some ideas that seemed weird at first, but they usually worked. For instance, he sent his players to an eye doctor, who helped them develop their hand-eye coordination. And he sent some of them to a power skating coach, who happened to be a woman, to help them improve their footwork.

The New York Islanders of the early 1980s were a very tight-knit group and very young (the average age of the players was only 26). But they had played together for a long time when they won their first Stanley Cup in 1980. Their road to the championship wasn't easy, however. Of the 21 playoff and championship games they played that year, six went into overtime.

The Islanders seemed to score goals in bunches. Their power play, which was when they had a man advantage because the other team had a player serving a penalty, was amazing in 1980. New York scored 15 power-play goals in the final series against the Philadelphia Flyers. The key player in the Islanders power play was Mike Bossy, who holds the record for most power-play goals in the playoffs in a career with 35. Bossy also holds the record for most power-play playoff goals in a season with nine.

In Game 1 of the 1980 Stanley Cup finals against Philadelphia, the Flyers scored first when Denis Potvin accidentally shot the puck into his own goal. With 3 minutes and 42 seconds left in the game, the Flyers were ahead 3–2. New York's Stephan Persson scored the tying goal with an assist from Bossy and Potvin on a power play. That sent the game into overtime.

Then Potvin made up for his first-period blunder by scoring the first power-play overtime goal in Stanley Cup history to give his team the win. Potvin had scored a hat trick (three goals in a game) of sorts during the game—he'd scored one goal for the Flyers and two for the Islanders!

The Flyers beat the Islanders 8–3 in the second game of the finals; but the Islanders bounced back on home ice in Game 3, winning 6–2. The fourth game was also played on the Islanders' home ice. While the crowd chanted, "We want the Cup!" the Islanders beat the Flyers 5–2, giving them a commanding 3–1 lead in the series. The game was close until the third period, when New York scored three goals (by Bryan Trottier, Bobby Nystrom and Clark Gillies) to put it away. Goal

The Islanders won their fourth Stanley Cup in 1983 when they swept the Edmonton Oilers.

tender Billy Smith won his 14th game of the playoffs, setting a new NHL record.

Game 5 was played in Philadelphia. The Islanders scored first, early in the game, on a power play goal by Stephan Persson, but Philadelphia scored, too. In the second period, the score was 2–2. From that point on, the game went completely the Flyers' way and the final score was Philadelphia 6, Islanders 3. But the Islanders still led the series three games to two, and that meant they only needed one more win to clinch their first championship.

In Game 6 at Long Island's Nassau Coliseum, New York was ahead

4–2 going into the third and final period. The Flyers kept skating hard and scored two quick goals to tie the score at 4–4. Seven minutes and eleven seconds into overtime, New York's Lorne Henning passed the puck to John Tonelli, who fed it perfectly to Bobby Nystrom. Nystrom *backhanded* the puck into the net behind Philadelphia goaltender Pete Peeters, winning the game and the series.

As team captain Denis Potvin lifted the 31-pound Cup over his head and skated around the rink followed by his teammates, 15,000 Long island fans went wild with joy.

In 1981, the Islanders had the most amazing power play in hockey history. They scored a record 31 goals in the Stanley Cup playoffs when they had a one-man or more advantage on the ice. In the finals against the Minnesota North Stars, they easily won the first three games of the series. They were unable to sweep the North Stars, and Minnesota won Game 4 in a 4–2 upset. Coach Arbour said, "Of course we wanted the sweep. But I know my team. They'll be ready for the next one."

And they were. The Islanders routed the North Stars in the fifth game of the series. The final score was 5–1 and the Islanders were Stanley Cup winners for the second year in a row. In '82 they beat the Vancouver Canucks four games straight in the finals and became the first U.S.-based team to win three consecutive Stanley Cups.

New York added a fourth Cup to its string by sweeping the final series in 1983 from the Edmonton Oilers. One of the most amazing things about the '83 Islanders was the balance of their scoring. Their first line (Trottier, Bossy and Anders Kallur) scored 17 goals. Their second line (Brent Sutter, Duane Sutter and Bobby Bourne) scored 21, and their third line (Nystrom, Butch Goring and John Tonelli) scored 18. Throughout the series the Islanders expertly killed penalties. This means they didn't let the Oilers score when New York had a man in the penalty box. In 20 power plays during the finals, the Oilers failed to score even once.

After winning the Stanley Cup for the fourth straight time, Denis Potvin exclaimed, "As far as I'm concerned, we're the best team to ever lace on skates!"

John McEnroe was a member of the U.S. Davis Cup team that lost only one match on its way to winning the Cup in 1979.

PRO TENNIS

BLOWIN' 'EM AWAY:
The 1979 United States
Davis Cup Team

There has never been a U.S. Davis Cup team like the team of 1979 (see Chapter 7 for an explanation of Davis Cup play). It included such star players as John McEnroe, Stan Smith, Vitas Gerulaitis and Bob Lutz, and lost only *one match* on its way to winning the Cup. McEnroe was the dominant player on the '79 team. In his first two years of Davis Cup competition, 1978 and '79, he didn't lose a set in either singles or doubles play. Though McEnroe is thought of as the "bad boy" of the tennis world because of his frequent displays of temper on the court, he loved to play in the Davis Cup. He didn't care that the money he might receive was nothing compared to the prizes awarded in tournaments held on the professional tour. McEnroe looked forward to playing for his country. He was inspired, and it showed in the way he played.

The opening round of the '79 tournament was held indoors in Cleveland, Ohio, and the U.S. defeated Colombia 5–0. In the second round, which took place the weekend after McEnroe had successfully defended his U.S. Open title against Gerulaitis, the American team faced Argentina. McEnroe and Gerulaitis, happy to be teammates again instead of opponents, were an unstoppable one-two punch. Gerulaitis lost only seven games to José-Luis Clerc, while McEnroe thrashed Guillermo Vilas.

The setting moved to Sydney, Australia for the next round. The most memorable match was between Gerulaitis and Australia's Mark Edmondson, and it was interrupted again and again by rain. There was a lot of wind as well, which made it difficult to control the ball, and the grass court was slippery and soggy. Edmondson, who was known to be tough when playing on grass, won the first two sets 8–6, 16–14 (play continued until one player won the set by two games). In the third set, with Gerulaitis serving, Edmondson was ahead 8 games to 7, and led 40–0. It was triple match point, which meant that all Edmondson had to do was win one more point in the next three opportunities and he would win the game, the set, and the match. What an upset that would have been! Gerulaitis was ranked fifth in the world, while Edmondson was ranked 73rd.

Though he was serving poorly, Gerulaitis charged the net aggressively and forced the Australian to make errors. Gerulaitis hit two winning volleys and then forced Edmondson to hit a backhand shot into the net. Edmondson became flustered, and Gerulaitis took charge, winning the next three sets 10–8, 6–3, 6–3, one after the other. The match lasted more than six hours, including more than three hours of rain delays.

Now the United States team was in the finals against the team from Italy. Never before had there been such a mismatch in the finals of Davis Cup play. To be fair, the Italians probably didn't have their minds entirely on tennis during those matches. Their captain, Umberto Bergamo, had been killed in a car crash the previous October, and the players hadn't yet recovered from the shock. Before the matches began, the members of the Italian team had many arguments among themselves debating whether their new captain should sit in Bergamo's chair, or if it should be left empty in his memory. This dispute also helped to destroy their concentration.

The Italians didn't have a lot of confidence, either. They played better on slow surfaces such as grass and clay, but the finals of that year's Davis Cup were played indoors in San Francisco's Civic Auditorium, and the surface was lightning fast. The Italians were afraid they didn't have the speed to keep up with the Americans, and they were right.

Just when things looked as if they couldn't get any worse for the Italian team, their star player, Corrado Barazzutti (bar-uh-ZOO-tee), twisted his ankle and had to pull out of his opening match against Gerulaitis, which he lost by default. McEnroe had no trouble defeating either of his opponents in his two singles matches. Gerulaitis won his other singles match, and the U.S. team of Smith and Lutz won the doubles competition.

Each member of the victorious American team received $50,000. Not bad, considering that they hardly had to break a sweat!

27

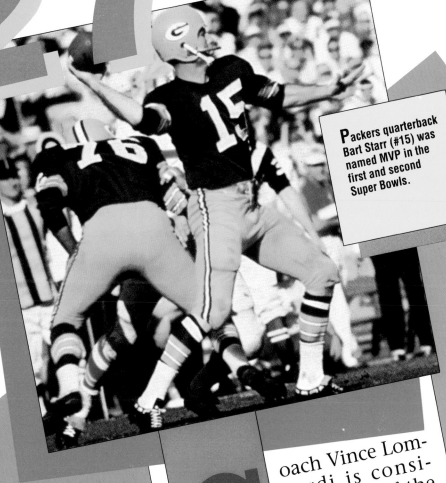

Packers quarterback Bart Starr (#15) was named MVP in the first and second Super Bowls.

PRO FOOTBALL

WINNING IS THE ONLY THING: Vince Lombardi's Green Bay Packers of the Mid-1960s

oach Vince Lombardi is considered one of the greatest football coaches of all time. In the mid-1960s, his Green Bay Packers won the first two Super Bowls, and fielded such terrific players as Bart Starr at quarterback, Paul Hornung and Jim Taylor at running back and Ray Nitschke at linebacker. While he was the Packers' coach, Lombardi was asked the secret of his success.

"It's simple," he replied. "I try to make each man on my team the best football player he can possibly be—and I try, and try, and try."

Lombardi was known for his hot temper both on and off the playing field, but he was able to use that temper effectively in his coaching. "If I yell at a player," he said, "I always do it for a reason. I make it clear that I'm yelling at a football player for his own benefit, as well as for the benefit of the team. I never carry a grudge."

When the Packers were in the midst of their dynasty, right defensive tackle Hank Jordan joked, "I'll say this for the coach. He treats us all the same—like dogs."

On January 15, 1967, in the Los Angeles Coliseum, the Green Bay Packers, the champion team of the NFL, played the Kansas City Chiefs—the American Football League (AFL) champions—in the very first Super Bowl before a small crowd of 62,000 spectators. The NFL had been the only professional football league in the U.S. for many years, and a lot of football fans didn't think much of the teams in the new AFL, which started in 1960. It was up to the Chiefs to prove that the AFL was equal to the NFL, and they tried. One thing was sure: The *leagues* may have been equal, but the Kansas City Chiefs were *not* equal to the Green Bay Packers.

There was no score in Super Bowl I until late in the first quarter, when Bart Starr threw a 37-yard touchdown pass to Max McGee. The Chiefs got their game together in the second quarter as quarterback Len Dawson picked apart the Packers secondary with a crisp passing game. He drove his team down the field and the Chiefs finally scored on a 16-yard pass from Dawson to Curtis McClinton. Then the Packers scored on a 14-yard touchdown run by Jim Taylor. The Chiefs answered back with a field goal. At halftime, the Packers led 14–10.

In the third quarter, the Packers hurried Dawson into throwing an interception. Willie Wood returned the ball to the Chiefs' 5-yard line and Elijah Pitts ran it in from there. The Packers never looked back. Final score: Green Bay 35, Kansas City 10. Bart Starr was named the first Super Bowl's MVP, completing 16 of 23 passes for 250 yards and 2 touchdowns, both to Max McGee.

The Packers' most famous game was played the following season. It was the 1967 NFL championship game against the Dallas Cowboys and it was the *coldest* football game ever played. The temperature in Green Bay, Wisconsin's Lambeau Field when the game began was 13 degrees below zero, and it had dropped to 15 below by the fourth quarter. Talk about home field advantage! The Packers, who were trying for their third straight NFL championship, knew all about playing in the cold. It's a lot colder in Wisconsin than it is in Dallas,

Texas, in December, and the Cowboys were in trouble from the start.

The Packers took a 14–0 lead early in the second quarter of what would come to be known as the "Ice Bowl." But the Cowboys came back, and Dallas defensive end Willie Townes sacked Bart Starr against the frozen ground. Starr fumbled the ball, and Cowboys George Andrie picked up the fumble, running for a touchdown. Later in the second quarter, Green Bay's Willie Wood fumbled a punt because his hands were numb with the cold. The Cowboys recovered the ball, and that turnover led to a 21-yard field goal for Dallas, making the score at halftime Green Bay 14, Dallas 10.

There was no score in the third quarter, but early in the fourth quarter the Cowboys ran a halfback option, a play in which the quarterback hands off the ball to the halfback, who then has to decide whether to run with the ball or pass it to a receiver downfield. Halfback Dan Reeves opted to throw the ball, and completed a 50-yard touchdown pass to Lance Rentzel.

With five minutes left to play in the game, the Packers had the ball for the last time. They started their drive on their own 31-yard line.

Packers coach Vince Lombardi (in raincoat) inspired his team to win, win, win.

By this time, icicles were hanging from the helmets of many of the players. On the last play of the game, Bart Starr scored the game-winning touchdown on a 1-yard quarterback sneak (the quarterback appears to hand the ball off but keeps it instead), making the final score 21–17. Vince Lombardi's Green Bay Packers had done it again!

Following their victory over the Cowboys in the Ice Bowl, the Packers thawed out and headed down to Miami, Florida's Orange Bowl for Super Bowl II against the Oakland Raiders from California. The Packers had a special reason for wanting to win that game aside from their desire to win two Super Bowls in a row. Vince Lombardi had announced that this would be his last season as their coach, and his team wanted him to go out a winner.

That Super Bowl was a defensive struggle for most of the first half. Late in the second quarter, the Packers led 6–0 on two Don Chandler field goals. Then lightning struck. The Packers had the ball, and Starr faded back to pass. The Raiders secondary fell apart, leaving Packers pass receiver Boyd Dowler wide open. Starr put the ball on his numbers and Dowler galloped in for a 38-yard touchdown.

Green Bay widened the lead in the second half, scoring on a touchdown run by Donny Anderson, a Chandler field goal and then an interception by Herb Adderley. The final score was Packers 33, Raiders 14. Bart Starr had completed 13 of 24 passes for 202 yards, and was again named the MVP.

The Packers had achieved both their goals. They had won two straight Super Bowls, and Coach Lombardi left in a blaze of glory, carried off the gridiron on the shoulders of his championship team.

CHAPTER 28

New York Mets pitcher Tom Seaver helped turn the '69 Mets from losers into winners.

BASEBALL

AMAZIN':
The 1969 New
York Mets

The '69 Mets were *amazing*, all right. When the season started, nobody expected them to win many games. But they did. In fact, they won the World Series.

The team was formed in 1962 when the National League expanded from 8 to 10 teams. As an expansion team, the '62 Mets were a combination of minor league ballplayers and aging veterans who many people thought should have retired long ago. The Mets were one of the worst baseball teams ever to take the field. Their manager was 71-year-old Casey Stengel. He had managed the Yankees from 1949 to 1960, winning 10 American League pennants and 7 World Series.

"Come see my amazin' Mets," he'd say. In 1962, they were amazing because of the many ways they knew how to lose! They lost their opening day game to the Cardinals 11–4, then lost the next eight games in a row. They finished the season with 40 wins and *120 losses*. The Mets seemed to be doing a comedy act, a comedy of errors, that is. Players forgot to touch bases. Outfielders dropped balls. Infielders threw to the wrong base. It seemed like every day the Mets came up with some new blooper.

In the next few years they didn't get much better. The Mets finished in last place in each of their first four years, and in 1965 Stengel retired. He was replaced by Wes Westrum. Under the new skipper, the team improved—a little. They finished ninth in the league in 1966, instead of tenth!

They finished last again in 1967, but for the first time there was a glimmer of hope. That was the first season for a young right-handed pitcher named Tom Seaver. Seaver won 16 games in '67 and was named Rookie of the Year.

In 1968, former Brooklyn Dodgers great (and former Met) Gil Hodges was named to manage the club, and things really started to change. The Mets got out of the cellar that season, finishing ninth again; but these were not the same Mets who had lost all those games in '62. These were quality ballplayers. Their pitching staff was strong and they began to look like winners.

Seaver won 25 games and lost 7 in 1969. His teammate, lefty Jerry Koosman, went 17–9. The other starters on the pitching staff were Gary Gentry, Jim McAndrew, Don Cardwell and Nolan Ryan (who won his 300th game in 1990 and is on his way to the Hall of Fame.)

There were only two strong hitters on the team, Cleon Jones and Tommy Agee. Agee hit 26 home runs in 1969 (batting leadoff!) and Jones batted .340, coming very close to winning the National League batting crown.

But the '69 season did not get off to a good start for the Mets. They lost their opener 11–10 to the Montreal Expos. On May 15, they lost a one-run game because of a base-running error by outfielder Art Shamsky. Near the end of May, they were beaten 15–3 by the Atlanta Braves and lost four more games in a row.

Then suddenly the tide turned. Behind Seaver's pitching, the Mets started to win. In June, they won 11 in a row. The team was actually

When the Mets won first place in the National League's Eastern Division, their fans were so excited that they stormed the field at Shea Stadium.

in second place in the Eastern Division. In first place were the Chicago Cubs, with superstars like Ernie Banks and Billy Williams and pitchers like Ken Holtzman and Ferguson Jenkins. In early July when the Cubs came to Shea Stadium, the Mets' new home in Flushing, New York, the underdogs cut the gap between them.

In the second game, Seaver retired 24 Cubs in a row and came within two outs of pitching a perfect game. The Mets ended up winning two out of three. Later that week, Gil Hodges began to talk to the press about his team's new winning attitude. "I'll tell you what's happening out there," he said. "When one guy lets down, another guy picks up for him. Everybody is winning games for us. You never know who'll be doing it next."

By September 8, the Mets were only 2½ games behind the Cubs. When the Cubs came to Shea again for a two-game series, the Mets won both games and then swept a doubleheader from the Expos on September 10. Something *really* amazing had happened. The Mets were in first place!

The team's pitching staff seemed to get better and better. In a doubleheader against the Pittsburgh Pirates, Koosman and Cardwell pitched back-to-back shutouts, both 1–0 victories. The Mets clinched a tie for first place in the Eastern Division on September 24, and the next night they won the Division outright behind a three-run homer by Donn Clendenon and a two-run homer by Ed Charles.

When the last out was recorded, 54,928 loyal Mets fans packing Shea Stadium went crazy. Some of them even ran out onto the field and started tearing up the turf for souvenirs. The players ran for safety into their clubhouse where they poured champagne over each other and shouted for joy.

In the National League playoffs, the Mets faced Hank Aaron and the Atlanta Braves of the Western Division in a three-game series. Nobody thought they could win—except the Mets. They swept the Braves 9–5, 11–6, 7–4. On to the World Series!

In the Fall Classic, the Mets were up against the Baltimore Orioles of the American League. Many people thought the Orioles were the best baseball team in years. They had two 20-game winners on their pitching staff, Mike Cuellar and Dave McNally, superstar Frank Robinson in the outfield and another Robinson, Brooks, at third.

The 1969 World Series opened in Baltimore. Tom Seaver started for the Mets, but he wasn't sharp and the Orioles won the first game 4–1. Jerry Koosman started Game 2 for the Mets and held the Orioles hitless for the first six innings. In the ninth inning, the Mets took a 2–1 lead that turned out to be the final score.

The Series moved to Shea Stadium for Game 3. The Mets won 5–0 behind the pitching of Gary Gentry. Their great pitching continued in the fourth game with Seaver on the mound. Until the ninth inning, the only run of the game had come on a homer by Clendenon in the second. Then, in the ninth inning, Baltimore tied the game 1–1. They would have gone ahead if it hadn't been for outfielder Ron Swoboda's backhanded catch of Brooks Robinson's sinking line drive to right center. That catch put the game into extra innings.

In the bottom of the 10th, Orioles outfielder Don Buford lost Jerry Grote's fly ball in the sun and Grote ended up with a double. Rod Gaspar, pinch-running for Grote, came around to score when reserve catcher J.C. Martin, pinch-hitting for Seaver, laid down a sacrifice bunt. The throw to first struck Martin and bounced away, allowing Gaspar to score the winning run. Later, a television replay showed that Martin had been inside the baseline in fair territory when the ball hit him. That meant that he should have been out, but none of the umpires had noticed — a lucky break for the Mets.

The Amazin' Mets finished off the Orioles in the fifth game, also in

Ed Kranepool poured champagne over manager Tug McGraw, celebrating the Miracle Mets' 1969 World Series victory.

New York. New York broke a 3–3 tie in the eighth when Jones and Swoboda had back-to-back doubles to help the Mets win the game 5–3. They had fought their way out of the cellar, finishing their season with a 100–62 record and as World Champions.

This time it wasn't just the fans at Shea who went crazy. The Mets' victory set off the biggest celebration New York City had ever seen. Schools suspended classes. Traffic all but stopped in downtown Manhattan during a tickertape parade to honor every member of the team. Famous violinist Isaac Stern said, "If the Mets can win the Series, anything can happen — even peace!"

Ron Swoboda summed it all up: "It's the first one and the sweetest, and because it's the first, nothing can ever be that sweet again."